In a thousand worlds, a thousand versions of me

chose you.

And where are those worlds now?

PAPER
ROAD
PRESS

This novel is entirely a work of fiction. The names, characters and incidents portrayed in it are the work of the author's imagination. Any resemblance to actual persons, living or dead, events or localities is entirely coincidental.

Paper Road Press
www.paperroadpress.co.nz

Published by Paper Road Press 2024

A catalogue record for this book is available from the National Library of New Zealand Te Puna Mātauranga o Aotearoa.

ebook ISBN 978-1-9911968-7-3 paperback 978-1-9911968-5-9

How to Get the *Girl* and Not Destroy the World

MARIE CARDNO

LAST TIME

"Was there ever a time when seeing the Endless didn't turn our brains to putty?" Sian asked absently, her hands far more focused than her words. Trillin wriggled, delighting in sensation.

"I don't remember," Trillin replied, almost as absently until her own words echoed inside her.

"Guess it isn't another spell, then."

"No – Sian, *I don't remember.* I should remember the first time the Endless saw a human screaming, but I don't. The memory isn't there. And if I don't have the memory…"

"Then the Endless doesn't, either. Huh." Sian rolled on top of her, arms braced either side of Trillin's form, eyes closed, with only a thin layer of skin between her and the terror they were discussing.

Trillin's body made a heart for itself without her even thinking about it; it made a heartbeat that hammered through everything she was.

"Hmm," Sian said. "What do you think? Should we give it a go? Saving the world?"

Saving the world. Saving *any* world. Something no part of the Endless had ever done before.

With the woman she loved.

The sun was sinking behind the mountains, taking the heat in the air with it. Trillin stared up at the woman lying over her, on her; the woman who'd risked her own soul to give Trillin a chance to be free.

Sian's heart was beating quickly, but it wasn't the frantic clutching at life that had frightened her so much back on that other Earth. Her skin was warm. The fine hairs on her arms and head moved like delicate fronds in the cooling breeze.

"We should attempt to save the world," Trillin said. "…Later."

This time, the kiss, and everything associated with it, went right.

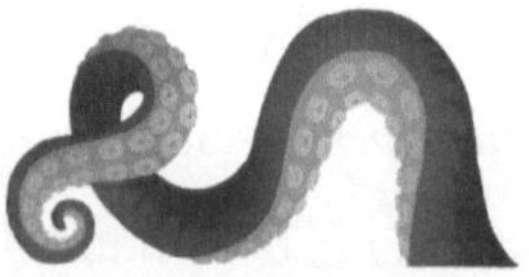

Kissing Trillin was … confusing.

And wonderful. Should that be the other way around? Wonderful and confusing. Not confusing and wonderful. The wonder was in every sensation, every heartbeat, every sound and shudder; the confusion was – well – "I need to *breathe*," Sian gasped reluctantly as she tried, again, to break away from Trillin's lips only to find another mouth pressing hungrily against hers.

"You can breathe through your nose." It sounded like a suggestion and a revelation at the same time, as though Trillin was that very minute delightedly realising noses were for breathing through. And it came from yet another mouth somewhere near the one on Sian's neck. Further down.

"Not when you're – *nggh*," Sian grunted. "What is that? A tentacle?"

"Here?"

"It *tickles*."

A brief pause, while the maybe-a-tentacle performed another shivering dance. "Does it tickle in a *good* way?" Trillin asked.

Sian had no fucking idea. It was taking all the mental capacity she had left even to remember to keep her eyes shut. One mistake, one glimpse of the wonderful woman wrapped and twisted around her, the monster who'd stolen her away and stolen the breath from her lungs, and she would lose more of her sanity than was already gone.

They were lying on tussock grass and hard dirt, dusk sprawling across the sky above. Trillin was a fragment of the Endless, eldritch and uncanny, but this was Sian's world. Her human mind would fracture and melt if she saw her here.

Would it be worth the terror of beholding her if it meant she *could* see her, like this? All mouths, all kissing, wanting and hungering and taking – her lungs burnt. She flung herself back, gasping, and for one exhilarating moment Trillin did not let her go. They'd started this with Sian straddling Trillin's then-humanoid form, but no human legs and arms could cage a shapeshifter who had to concentrate to keep her edges solid; Trillin had clung and melted around and over her, hot and inquisitive, exploring and enveloping.

Trillin released her. Sian's chest heaved. Oxygen woke her brain up, a bit, and the shot of mental clarity hit like a boot to the chest.

"I wish I could see you," she groaned.

"Careful." A tendril twisted in her palm, stretching her fingers out and winding around them. "Remember what a wish did in that other world."

Sian blew out her cheeks. "Fucked it up for everyone, you mean?"

The memory sobered her better than oxygen. They'd only just returned from that other Earth, where all the world's magic was devoured by a single death-empowered enchantment that twisted people to enact its vision of a happy ending.

She shook her head. "It wouldn't happen here. That wish had so much power because the enchanter died making it."

"Is a dying wish more powerful than a living one?"

"Is – what?" Sian's lips twitched up. Now she *really* wished she could see her – Trillin's voice was all innocent curiosity, but Trillin was so much more than her voice. Her emotions played over her entire body, *remade* her body, and half of understanding her was seeing joy or excitement or discovery burst over her skin.

Or fear.

She frowned, and Trillin was there, smoothing her brow with a slinking softness. "In times of great distress, the magician's natural powers are honed to a sharpness and intensity that should strike fear into any right-thinking man's heart," she recited. "Part of what I am remembers that, now. I should have remembered earlier."

"Where did you hear that?"

A hesitation – then a surging shrug beneath her hands. A prickle of changing texture. Not fear, not exactly, but something close.

"Can't have done them much good, whoever said it," Sian blustered, trying to push the subject aside. "If the Endless got them anyway."

Trillin stilled and curled in on herself. "It didn't do him any good at all. He was remembering it when the Endless took him. Trusting in it to be true."

Bloody hell. If catching her breath hadn't already cooled down other parts of her body, that would have done it. Why were they talking about this? "That's depressing."

"He was thinking about sex, too."

Sian almost choked. "What?"

"He was trying to think only of his death, and the power that came with it, but he kept thinking, *What if the sexual release was a distress as great as death*? And *Why hadn't he tried it instead*? And *Why am I thinking this now, oh god oh god oh god.*"

"Tried it right when—" Sian swore. "And that's the sort of thing that goes through the Endless's mind now, instead?"

Trillin's laughter was a physical force, trembling across Sian's skin where they touched. "No. It doesn't hunger in that way. All those thoughts and memories and longings … they belong to it, now, but it doesn't understand them."

She splayed too-long fingers over Sian's stomach, and Sian thought she began to understand.

"But you do?"

"I kissed you until you could not breathe," Trillin reminded her with a hint of sternness. "I wanted to keep kissing you until you swooned, but I did not. You are still recovering from the other world."

"Not that slowly," Sian argued. "Anyway, if you're worried about me wishing up something by accident as I pass out, don't. There's not enough magic in me yet to hone into anything."

"This world is healing you," Trillin breathed, her voice a chorus sending shivers across Sian's skin.

"Rolling around in the dirt helps," Sian admitted, and grimaced. Trillin traced the expression.

"That makes you unhappy?"

"It's a bit embarrassing?" Which shouldn't have been a question, but came out like one.

"Why?"

Sian had no answer for her.

"Perhaps—" The word flew into the air between them, and then in a surge Trillin gathered it up and kept speaking. "Perhaps it is like – me."

"Like you?"

"Not *here*, not anymore – not me, really, but – the Endless takes the world into itself, and makes it something new. Makes itself something new, made of what it takes." She squirmed, as though something not herself had gotten under her skin. Or something uncomfortable that *was* herself. "I try not to now, but – no, I was saying that you are like that, so it is not a *bad* thing, but it is…"

"You made yourself something new, too," Sian reminded her. "More new than the Endless, no matter how much it eats. That thing hasn't changed the whole time my lot have known about it. Centuries."

"I made myself out of it." Trillin's voice was a fading whisper. "Whatever it was, it was something I could make myself from."

"And I'm making myself of the grass and dirt?" Sian joked. Trillin's quietness worried her, and she held her closer. "Maybe that isn't such a bad thought. I mean, not dirt exactly, but … did I explain digestion to you, in the end? Not that I really know how that works, either…"

Her mind was leaping away. Dirt and grass and magic. A world that nourished her in a way she didn't even notice until she was starved of it. She'd been soaking in magic since she could remember: her aunt's garden, the bush around the hills, the beach. Mushroomy student accommodation. When had it become embarrassing?

Anyway, she did fucking love this place. The bleached hillsides, the white burn of the sun. The same as she loved the green and damp of other parts of it, the cloaks of snow and clouds at the peaks and the ocean a devouring mouth all around.

Hmm.

Maybe she shouldn't interrogate that too much.

Trillin was still following her own winding thoughts. Or maybe Sian was the one who'd wandered off, while Trillin managed to stay still.

"Is it strange that we are so different, still, after so long?" Trillin said thoughtfully. "So much of what I am is … what your people were."

Sian rolled onto her stomach, propping her chin on her hands. "Not my people," she said, back on solid genealogical ground. "None of my dead ever made it to your world. I mean, personally."

"But what I was made it to yours."

"Through holes witches here dug in the fabric of realities we didn't understand. I tried mapping earlier expeditions, before I found you. No trace of them by the time we were looking." She paused. "Except … except another way of looking at it, it was all trace. Everything they were, was still in there somewhere."

Something tugged at her conscience and, hell, she wasn't sure how she felt about having one of those. All these adventures with Trillin – she was learning too much about herself.

She had to ask. If she didn't it would roll around in her head, snowballing until it was all she could think about. "What do you think happened back there after we left?"

Trillin didn't need to ask what *back there* meant. She followed Sian over the conversational train tracks as easily as Sian's own mind jumped them. "To the magic in the other Earth, after you broke the spell?"

"To all of it. Everyone. Would it be worse to leave them alone, or worse to go and check? We left Bunny there. That's barely a bloody metaphor. Invasive species aren't all happy fun times for the places they invade..."

She trailed off.

"What should we do now?"

She reached for Trillin and found a form that, beneath her hand, became firm and solid enough to pull on top of her.

"What was it we said earlier? Something about saving the world?" She let her head drop back. "I'm still tired. So maybe that can wait a bit, until..."

"Later?" The hint of teasing in Trillin's voice was a tangible thing, whispering across Sian's skin.

LATER

Later came way too fucking fast. Which was something Sian could sympathise with, apparently. News to her. She was full of self-discoveries today. Hopefully, the next one would be less embarrassing.

They were resting, because she suddenly wasn't in the mood to jump up and do the next thing, even if the next thing was saving the world. No. Because she needed to *rest.* Another revelation she wasn't sure she was in the mood for, thank you, universe.

"We should—" she began, and groaned, because no good thing ever came of saying *we should.* But there was a new energy beneath her skin, a familiar urgency. Not an urgency for anything in particular, just a push-push-push of *come on, let's go, let's find something to do...*

It always pushed her towards the Endless, before. But – seriously? *Now?* When she had the best part of it already in her arms?

"You have your fill of magic again, and you're too restless to stay in one place?" Laughter lilted along Trillin's form.

"You can tell?" Sian hesitated. "Is that what it is?"

"I can't see it. Not the way I see your skin, or hair. It's like your bones," Trillin thrummed, delighted with the parallel. "You must have bones, because I can see the effects of them, in holding your body to their shape. But I cannot see *them.* Um. Unless I make eyes that can. And your magic – I cannot see it. But when you sicken without it – I *can* see that. And now..."

Tendrils quested out across Sian's face, soft and seeking.

"I look better?" Sian suggested.

"You always look wonderful. But now you look well again, too. Like when we first met."

Heat shot to her cheeks and Trillin's touch became more inquisitive, tracing how far the blush went. Ears, jaw, throat. "When we first met?" Sian managed, her voice strangled.

The first time she'd seen Trillin and known it was Trillin she was seeing, she'd jumped through a portal into an alien dimension, with nothing but a spelled harness and a ten-dollar bet that she'd make it back alive between her and certain death.

A death that would have made her a part of the monster Trillin had built herself out of.

She shook away the thought. "You looked pretty good, too."

"I didn't even have *legs*," Trillin protested.

"Not sure you have legs now, either, let's be fair."

A rush of air, and she was on her back, Trillin above her. Sun-crisped grass rustled; a tentacle grasped her by the wrist, pulling her hand to a smooth expanse of skin stretched over carefully crafted bone and muscle.

"*This* is a leg," Trillin declared triumphantly.

"Can't argue with that." Sian pulled her down.

Forget about *should.* Forget about the urgency humming in her blood. She was home. They had all the time in the world.

And the world was the right one. The sky above was the sky she'd grown up beneath. The air was the air she'd taken her first breath in. The tussocks bent beneath her and waving golden all around were – well, she'd probably never rolled around in these particular tussocks before, but they were lush and prickly with the magic she needed as much as the blood rushing through her veins, so they fitted, too.

She fitted.

Her world.

And yet…

Her eyelids twitched, a blink without her eyes ever being open. Something wasn't right.

She pushed herself up on her elbows. The sun had crept away while they were busy, like it didn't want to make a fuss, and the last of the day's warmth had crept with it. She wasn't cold yet. Warm from relief, warm from being with Trillin, warm from discovery and joy and the sort of sex she wouldn't have thought possible, if she'd given much thought to it beforehand. Strong evidence in favour of not thinking things through in advance, really.

This world was *her* world, so while they'd been rolling around in the grass her body had done its thing and sucked in enough magic to keep her from coming apart at the seams.

But something wasn't right. More curious than wary, she turned to where she thought Trillin wasn't and opened her eyes.

The world swam around her. Not all of it was the world, of course.

She'd misjudged her direction. Some of it was her girlfriend. A thousand thousand glinting lights like something from the bottom of the ocean; countless tiny threads and fronds, tentacles so fine a breath sent them boiling away like ink in clear water.

Her throat tightened. Terror bloomed like plasma behind her ribs, burning her breath away so that by the time she opened her mouth to scream she would have no air left to scream with.

"Trillin," she croaked, sliding in a moment before the screaming began.

Matter coalesced. The shimmer-mist of tendrils flicked away out of sight, and then behind her, Trillin's drifting contentment pulsed itself into something that could form a mouth. "Is that better?"

She could breathe again. But she could see what Trillin's body had been hiding. All those wheeling stars.

"Trillin, look up there." She got to her feet, blinking as black pulled in at the edges of her vision. "The sky. Something's—"

Strange, she was about to say.

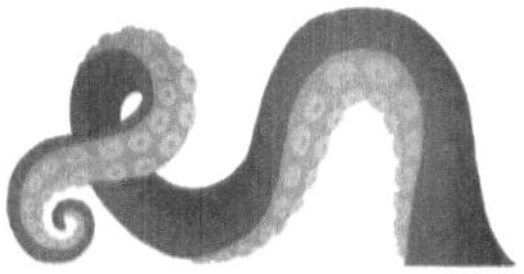

Sian blinked.

"I don't remember," Trillin said, then – "Sian, be careful!"

For one moment that cracked her mind in two, she'd stared directly into Trillin's eyes. Twin galaxies stared back: whorls of starlight and dust and life staring shocked into her face with more concern than actual worlds ever showed anyone.

Terror coursed through her. The concern frightened her more than not being noticed at all – it meant it saw her, it knew where she was, there was no escape – Trillin slapped an appendage over her face.

"What happened?" Sian asked, closing her eyes behind the fleshy blindfold. "Why'm I on the ground again?"

"We're back in your world." A cautious tendril found the pulse in her neck, tested it against the hammering in her chest and her wrists. "You – there is so much magic in you, already. I thought it would take longer."

"Take longer? We've been here for hours. All afternoon, all night."

There was a pause. "Not *that* many hours." Trillin's voice had the hesitation of someone remembering someone else's memories of how timekeeping worked. "It hasn't been night yet."

"What?" She struggled upright and that felt – familiar, in a way that lurched. Pushing up to her elbows. Standing up. What had – hadn't she—? "What were you saying just now? You didn't remember?"

"You asked me if the Endless remembered the first time it encountered someone from your world, and I … don't remember." Her grip on Sian trembled, and something inside Sian trembled, too. "Sian, *I don't remember.*"

Sian recited the words silently along with her as she said them again with the same cresting amazement she had the first time, hours ago, when the sun was still up.

The sun that was still warm on her skin now.

"I should remember the first time the Endless saw a human screaming, but I don't. The memory isn't there. And if I don't have the memory…"

"Then the Endless doesn't, either," Sian repeated, feeling like she was reading from a script. That was what she'd said the last time, wasn't it? The last time she'd … been in this time…

Her lips froze on the next words.

What do you think? Should we give it a go? Saving the world?

"Something went wrong," she said instead. "We've done this before. We've *been* here before. You don't remember?" She reached out until she found something that resolved into the face Trillin chose most often for her to touch – long elegant lines, the hint of a jawbone, a mouth to meet the pad of her thumb and coiling lashes to brush against her fingertips. Too many eyes by human standards, but who cared about that?

The last time around—"You don't remember *any* of it?" she asked, stung by the plaintive note in her own voice.

"What is there to remember?" Trillin blinked against her little finger. "What do you mean, we've been here before?"

"We've had this conversation already. We've – I've – been *here* already. In this time. You saved me. I carked it on the ground for a bit, absorbing magic … We talked about the Endless not remembering the first time it encountered a human, and about saving the world, and then we – uh—"

"Then we what?"

How was she meant to answer that?

"Uh," she began, leaving her mouth open for any number of suave utterances to utter themselves. None did, the bastards.

Trillin was all muscular strength and experimental joints, the monster who'd ripped through worlds to steal her away. No hint of the unravelled bliss that had started with their kiss.

The kiss they hadn't even *had*, if she really had jumped back in time. The kiss there was no trace of ever existing, except in her memory.

Let alone everything else.

She could remember, and Trillin couldn't.

That was fucked up, right? Super fucked.

"Something felt different, *wrong*, and then—" She twisted to look up at the sky.

Trillin's tentacle tightened over her eyelids. "Wait!"

Sian waited. Trillin was mostly silent as she moved – a bit squelchy – but she reconstituted herself, pressed to Sian's back, a solid torso and limbs that held her but would be out of sight when she opened her eyes. Sian let her head fall back.

Trillin carefully retracted her blindfold tendril. "Ready."

Sian lay in her arms and stared at the sky.

"It was hours later than this," she said quietly, gazing up at the first stars to break through the fading blue. "Full dark. No clouds. And the stars were broken. Every single one, cracked in pieces, and then I opened my eyes and was back here again."

"Are you sure?" Trillin touched her forehead, the pulse in her throat. "That other world weakened you very badly. You need time to recover and we only just arrived here. You've been lying here with me the whole time."

Sian let her words fall like raindrops on her thoughts, resisting the instant urge to dash them away. What was Trillin suggesting? That she'd made it up? It *had* happened. She remembered it all. But…

Sometimes, with magic, certainty was all that kept you going. And sometimes it was what got you totally fucked, as you marched confidently into a hole filled with spikes.

Had she imagined it? Dreamed it?

She'd had worse dreams.

Though she was sure even her sleeping mind couldn't have come up with some of the things that had happened in this one.

Sian shook her head. "I'm sure. You said it yourself, just now. I've absorbed more magic than I should have if we just got here."

"That is true." Trillin's explorations paused. "But how is that possible?"

She winced, because she really didn't want to be the one to suggest this. "Time magic?"

Time magic. Of all the subjects she never bothered with because why would you? It wasn't as though anyone knew if it ever *worked.* Various academics had come out with books on the subjects over the years, but they all basically came down to saying, *Look, the world as you know it isn't the world as it was BEFORE my amazing breakthrough in chronomancy, and I can prove it because see how we're not all being overrun by whatever monster is most exciting to people of the specific era I'm writing in, ooh, aren't you all glad I saved you, tenure please.*

Most of those books had been assigned texts for one course or another in undergrad, and she'd pretty much written them off as made up. It wasn't as though anyone could peer review them. She'd been more interested in the Endless by then, anyway. The same way everyone in the department ended up pulled to it.

The Endless. Even the thought of it plucked at her, at the restless energy of her magic. Was this related to it somehow? Or was she just coming up with more excuses to poke holes in the world?

Honestly. The magic in that other Earth had been weird as fuck, but now she was back home, home wasn't exactly covering itself in normality either.

She scrubbed her hands over her face. "Time magic. Has to be, right? Some sort of a loop, and we popped back here. Um, a localised dislocation? I have all the magic that my body already absorbed from my previous location in the timeline then, so this must still be my same body. I haven't shunted backwards in time into a previous version of myself—"

"You *are* the same." Trillin was indignant and – argh, if only she could look at her and *see* the shade of upset she was. "Every part of you."

"Except the parts that were previously dying of magical starvation." She drew a shaky breath. "Trillin, you don't have to believe me, but I need to know for sure, okay?"

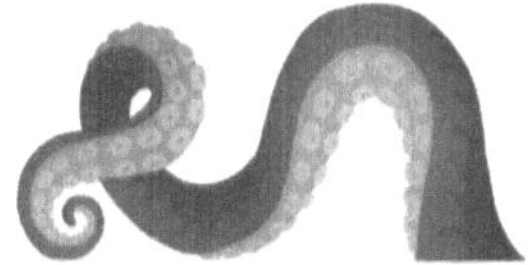

The evening slipped away less pleasantly than the last time. Sian put her newly rehydrated magic to use, trying to find some physical trace of whatever had happened.

"I just want to say I never claimed to be great at this," she said as the latest attempt collapsed into itself, revealing absolutely nothing about the continuous or non-continuous nature of time but leaving a taste of rancid butter in the air.

"Or perhaps you are not finding anything because there is nothing to find." Trillin wrapped a warning tendril around her wrist, and Sian closed her eyes and waited for her to come closer.

Grass shivered behind her as Trillin moved. Still the Trillin of firm edges and determination, not the one she'd left behind, all gossamer and wispy. Her heart twisted. Still the *same* Trillin, still the monstrous woman she'd stolen away from her own dimension and who had stolen her in turn … but a Trillin a handful of hours earlier. A handful of hours that passed in different ways. Did that change things?

Trillin approached slowly, hesitantly. No touch, other than that ribbon around her wrist, only the hint of warmth against her skin that meant Trillin was close to her and raising her body's temperature enough for Sian to feel it.

"You still don't believe me." Sian grimaced. "Look, I know all these experiments haven't proved anything, but—"

"There could be another explanation for what you are experiencing." Trillin's voice was halting, pulled along by something that felt like another echo of someone else's thoughts. "No part of the Endless has spent as much time with a human as I have with you. No human has ever spent days with the Endless without being … altered."

"You think being together has made me lose my mind? But I haven't been looking at you. Much. Not since we figured out that if I just kept my eyes shut, things stayed fine."

"We do not know if that is true." Heat sizzled in Trillin's voice, her larynx transforming into something sharp-edged with guilt. "We do not know that you are *fine.* I took you to a world that almost killed you, I let us both be taken over by an entity that wanted us to kill one another—"

"That wasn't your fault," Sian hurried to reassure her. "You couldn't have known that world would be like that. Neither of us had ever seen an enchantment that fed on itself like that."

"I was part of the Endless! I am the one that is meant to take over, not be taken!" Trillin surged, a tide of helpless rage. "The Endless fed on countless minds, minds that *knew* magic of the type we encountered, and—"

"Sex."

The word broke through Trillin's boiling anger. "Y-yes?" a thousand lips mouthed.

"You told me. Last time around, before I looped back in time. Someone the Endless ate – the last thing he thought was whether his dying wish could do some sort of big magic, but he got distracted and started thinking about whether sex could do it, too. I mean, probably not, right? If sex could supercharge spells like that we'd all be at it like—"

The kiss was like being bowled by surf. Trillin lifted her up and tossed her around, spray and mist and all the relentless power of the ocean. When she fell back, Sian was gasping.

"But what if it is true? What if you don't need to look at me to be terrorised – if just being around each other…" Tendrils like seaweed rolling underwater clung to her, then peeled away. "If all this is only hurting you…"

"That isn't it. It *can't* be it. I'm not imagining what happened – time repeated itself." A sliver of doubt wormed its way through Sian's mind, but she ignored it. "There's nothing wrong with me. It's the world that's – look, time magic is complicated."

"Then why don't I know about it? Why has no human the Endless ever eaten thought to turn back time?"

"Because—" Her rebuttal fell away. "Look, there's one more thing I want to try. Let's—"

She glanced up by chance. Or maybe some part of her had clocked the time.

Above them, the stars splintered into a thousand broken shards.

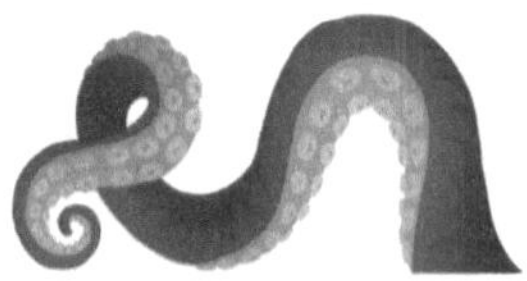

Again.

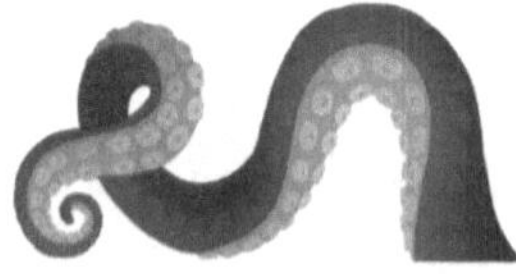

Again.

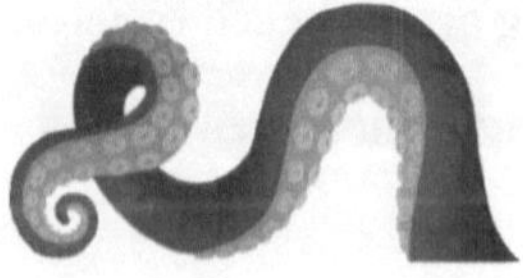

"Please tell me you got it did time. We keep coming back," Sian blurted the moment the world came back into focus.

"Back where?"

"Back here."

Trillin's voice had at least one smile in it. "Back to your world, yes. Are you feeling better?"

"I feel like I'm on a fucking merry-go-round." Sian rubbed her eyes. "You really don't feel—"

She broke off. Was she going mad? It was a probability. It was always a probability, alongside just straight up dying.

Okay. First things first. Trillin had just said she didn't remember the Endless first encountering humans, blah blah blah. Then she would say something about saving the world.

"What do you want to do next?" she asked instead.

"Do we have to do anything?"

Sian stared at where Trillin's voice was, eyes closed against the glorious horror.

Did they have to do anything? Did she have to keep trying, over and over?

"Okay. It's worth a try."

They stayed right where they were, exhausting one another and all the possibilities of shape-changing limbs and sensual sensory overload, and then—

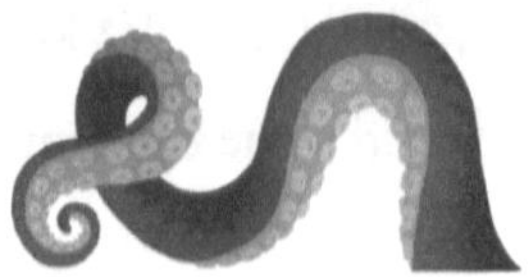

Sian lifted her head to find the tussock swaying unflattened around them, no prickles in her knees, that one big flat convenient-height rock still all the way over there.

"FUCK!"

It hadn't even been a theory until it was almost too late, but here was another option to cross out: no orgasm-wishing their way out of the time loop.

Next plan.

She reached for Trillin. "Let's go somewhere else. Can we still do that?"

Confusion buffeted around Trillin as soft wings. "We just arrived—"

"I'm all better. Fuelled up and ready to go. There's a whole universe out there, isn't there? Let's go find it."

They found it. Trillin unpicked the seams of the universe for her and they visited a thousand distant stars, worlds like and unlike her own Earth, atmospheres breathable and some so toxic Trillin had to wrap herself around Sian in a protective envelope until she could get them both somewhere else.

Over and over.

One trip at a time, and each trip was the first time. Sian raised her head from tussock grasses waving gently in the breeze like nobody ever fucked in them or braided them into stupid little crowns or accidentally tracked acidic purple mud onto them.

"What were we saying?" she asked tentatively.

And the same conversation flowed over her, the same way it had so many times before.

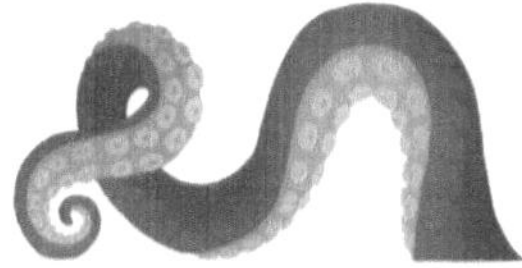

There had to be somewhere the loop wouldn't get them. Whatever was causing it.

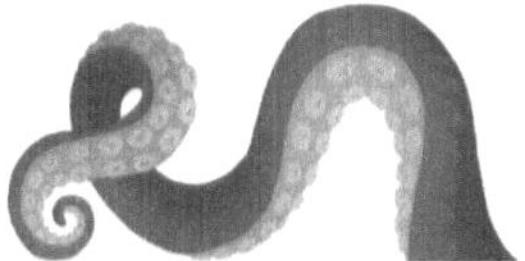

That was a thought. Was it a *thing* after them? Was time itself in a loop, for the entire universe, or were they trapped in some sort of catch-and-release enchantment that kept releasing her in the wrong moment? Was there more going on than she remembered? Was she missing pieces of what was happening to them, the same way Trillin was missing her memories each time they came back to the same place?

They tried so many places. The copy-cat world, alien planets, the heart of a magical explosion so intense Trillin used the explosion's own power to build another bubble-sanctuary around them, the same as the one the dragon had crushed on that other Earth.

They avoided other Earths. Sian gave up explaining why.

Nothing worked.

Was it happening to both of them, and only Sian could remember each repeat, or was it only happening to her?

One way to test that.

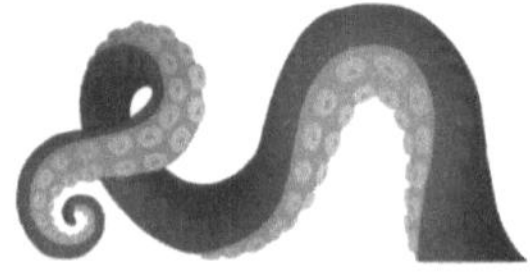

Trillin thought she'd lost her bloody mind and, honestly, Sian couldn't be sure she was wrong.

"I don't know whether something is targeting us or it's a natural phenomenon we're both stuck in. But if it's only me – if you could get out of it if only you weren't right there with me – we have to know."

"Sian, wait. You aren't—"

Trillin tried to argue, but Sian had been paying attention when she built all those portals all those last times. She twisted magic around herself, etching out the break points like the dotted rip lines on an old sheet of stamps, and cut herself out of the world before Trillin could hold onto her.

And when the sky broke above her that time, she had no one to hold onto.

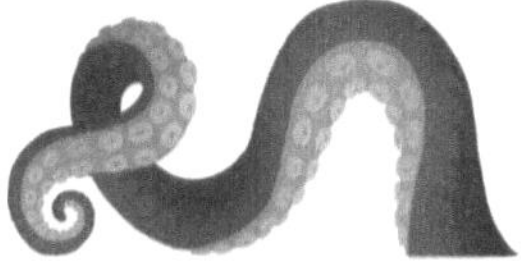

The bed of tussock grass, again. The last warmth of the sun before it crept behind the mountains on the horizon, again. The rocky tors like broken teeth pushing though golden hills. Again.

And Trillin.

She tumbled into her, grasping and possessive, eyes open because at least the terror meant they were both still here.

Trillin slapped a tentacle over her eyes. "What are you doing?"

"I—" Her throat dried up. She'd given up explaining, how many attempts ago?

Why was she even bothering? She wasn't good at this sort of thing. The throwing herself into danger, yes; the planning and theorising and coming up with a plan that made sense, that *worked*? No. She needed other people for that. Always had.

"Something is wrong." Trillin held her gently, became a gentle thing for her to hold, checking Sian's body for injury and exhaustion the way she had a dozen times already, but as tentatively as though it was the first. Because for her it was. The first time, again. Always again. "What happened?"

"It's not what happened. It's what's going to happen." She drew a ragged breath. How had she argued this with Trillin all the times before she gave up? "Look, this isn't going to make any sense, and I don't have any proof of it, but we're caught in some sort of time loop. We keep coming back here. Or I do. You're always here, but you don't remember."

"I don't remember—"

"And you just said you don't remember, but you were talking about – oh, shit – you were talking about the Endless not having its first memory of encountering humans – but this is different, you don't remember—"

"*Breathe.*"

The word hummed in her bones. She inhaled, slow and uneven against the hammering of blood in her ears.

"You've travelled through time. Lived these moments over and over? How many times?" Trillin asked.

"I – what – you believe me?"

"Yes."

The next breath was easier to take. She wanted to look at Trillin – she always wanted to look at her. Why did they always have to come back here, where she couldn't? – but instead she squeezed her eyes shut behind her tentacle blindfold.

"Why?" she asked bluntly.

Because Trillin had never believed her before. And they were back to the beginning. She hadn't tried any new way to convince her. Why would she believe her now?

"Because of you. You are … different." A tendril curled on her cheek. "You have never changed like I do, and I love you for that. But you do change, slowly, cell by cell. And I have missed some of it." Worry painted the undercurrents of her voice. "You are not the same as you were when we started talking. Only moments ago."

She believes me. How many resets? She'd lost count. And now Trillin believed her without question.

Because all those resets were starting to show on a cellular level.

"Okay," she gulped. "Well, that's good and bad, I guess."

"We must stop it from happening again." Trillin hesitated. "How many times have you been through this?"

"I lost count."

"And each repeat is…?"

"A few hours. The same few hours." Panic bubbled up inside her again, but she swallowed it back. It was easier to hide it, now Trillin knew. No point keeping up appearances when the woman you loved already thought you'd lost your mind, but when she knew you were telling the truth and was as worried as you were?

It was as though a weight lifted from her shoulders.

And landed directly on Trillin's.

"But it's fine," she said, fooling herself that Trillin wouldn't sense the tremor in her voice. "Kind of exciting, right? The same few hours happening over and over again. What could we do with an opportunity like that? You could do anything, knowing the reset will put things back the way they were. It's – I mean, time magic's illegal, but the sort of illegal where if you do it right, who's going to know?"

Trillin waited a beat after she finished talking. "Did that sound more convincing in your head before you said it out loud?"

"…No."

"Whatever is happening does not reset everything. I have not experienced the extra time you have. But *you have.* Whatever happens to you in these hours before you come back, you bring back with you."

"I mean, yeah, but…" She leant against where she figured Trillin was, and found her there, a steady trunk and arms boneless but strong around her. "It's more fun to think, ooh, illegal magic hijinks than that at some point I'll zap back here and I'll be hurt. Or old. Or more insane than I feel already, or dead, and you'll think you did something wrong bringing me back here. You'll think you saved me from that happy-ever-after curse and it made me lose my mind."

"You say that as though you've heard it before."

She laughed hollowly. "You thought me just being with you had made me mad," she told her. "I don't want that to happen again. Not if I won't be here to tell you you're wrong."

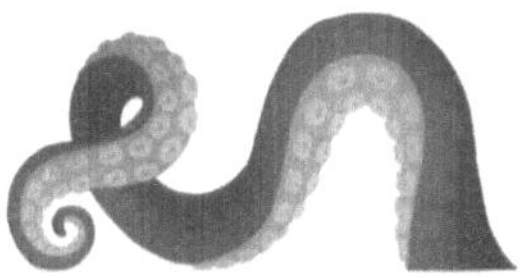

If Sian was telling the truth, then this was not the first time Trillin had turned all her eyes on her and found her changed.

She held her edges with care; beneath, everything else that she was boiled and hissed with fear.

If they did not fix this, the next version of herself would not remember that thought. Would not remember this Sian, changed but still herself, older and with her magic replenished but her mind strung tight ready to snap.

She twisted the memory into a knot, buried it deep within herself, as though that would help when this version of herself had never existed. When some future past version of herself turned to Sian and found her wasted away in her arms.

Sian would be dead, and she would not know why.

"You'll think it's your fault." Sian's voice was weary-angry. "And I wish I could tell you now that it won't be and have you remember then, but I can't. I've already – it doesn't work that way. Trust me on this." Her head drooped. "But if we can fix it…"

Sian was a crackling flame of determination, and Trillin couldn't help but wind herself around her as she planned out-loud how they could evade or take advantage of the time resets. Her beloved burnt, and she warmed herself on that proof of her life – recovered from the magic starvation that had parched her in the other Earth, but already with too many charred pieces.

A fire and what the fire had already burnt, at the same time. Sian's voice was ragged as she listed all the things she had already tried. All the trimmed-away hours that Trillin had lost of her.

Sian talked, and Trillin investigated, cataloguing the changes she had already noticed. Hair infinitesimally longer. Skin drier, a thin, red rash along the back of one arm. Acid? The muscles of her face pinched in new ways around the eyes and mouth, etching unfamiliar lines.

Her muscles held her bones too tightly.

Trillin could fix that. It was a problem easily dealt with from the inside. Less so, from without. And not easy in either direction for Sian, perhaps. But she could help. She loved Sian's slow changes the way she thrilled at the slow changes that stirred her world – but not like this. These changes – she wanted to stop them. Reverse them.

With slow, gentle strength she kneaded the deep knots in Sian's shoulders.

"Trillin? Babe? It's a bit hard to think when you're doing that."

Sian's eyes were carefully closed, but even without their wondrous sheen Trillin could trace the pleasure in her face.

"There'll be time for that later." Her mouth twitched – a smile, caught before it could escape. "Or before this is over, again, maybe."

"*Again*?" A frisson of outrage sizzled through her, and Sian laughed and leant into her in exactly the spot to make her melt and close herself around her. Her Sian, her wondrous human who could not even look at her without screaming, but who knew her shapes and chosen contours so well.

She discovered something new and all to herself: that Sian knew parts of Trillin better than she knew them herself, and that knowing it was a comfort.

And if time reset again, she would lose it. Forget Sian being this way, forget herself being this way.

Trillin was familiar with panic. The human minds that had fed the Endless throughout the ages knew it intimately, and she plucked through their memories, finding reverberations of the fear that took over Sian's mind when she looked at Trillin.

Those memories were nothing like experiencing it herself, an emotion, a physical presence like a parasite birthing itself, clawing and scrape-edged beneath her skin.

"What can we do?" she asked out loud.

"Same thing I've been doing for – however long it's been? I mean it's working so well already." Sian groaned and scruffed at her hair. "No. There has to be something else. We can't escape it – but there must be something I'm missing."

"It does not leave any trace on the fabric of your world?"

Sian's mouth twisted oddly. "Nope. Everything goes back the way it was. I mean, everything stays the way it was."

"Everything that *you* can sense," Trillin suggested hesitantly.

Sian's spine straightened. The breath that left her lungs turned her mouth into a smile. "Yes! I'm limited by what *I* can sense. Can you—?"

"I shall try."

Trillin took Sian's hand. She made a hand for herself to do it; carefully jointed, tendons and ligaments beneath skin that sighed against Sian's warmth. An anchor as she undid the rest of herself.

Every atom of her being was a victory of her individual self against the Endless. She had stolen them one by one while the leviathan mind fixed its primary attentions elsewhere. As she became enough of herself to be daring, she'd taken a scatter or a handful at a time, building herself from everything she had been a part of before.

She had let none of it go. The Endless was profligate with its fragments; she could not risk a single one. Whatever she let go could not be replaced without returning to the Endless itself to steal more.

Or devouring the world she found herself in now.

She whisked her mind away from the thought, leaving it to hang dark and cold and then disintegrate as she unfolded most of herself into a searching expanse of sensory organs.

Other thoughts whispered up as she focused her senses outwards. Sian did not share her wariness of losing parts of her body. Small parts, at least. Hair. Skin. Sweat and spit, the moisture that travelled into her body and out again. Sian replenished her body from the world around her, and parts of her became parts of it in turn.

"What are you looking for?" Sian asked.

Trillin explained, her mouth soft against Sian's wrist.

"You're looking for my *dandruff*? Actually that's a brilliant idea. *I'm* coming back each time, but what counts as me? If my DNA or whatever I've shed—"

"There's nothing." No trace of Sian in the world around them, except what was still a part of her whole and living body.

"Oh."

Trillin searched farther. She knew what this world should feel like, from the memories she'd taken with her from the Endless. Its taste, its textures, its chill and stillness and startling changes. The roar of the distant sun beneath the horizon.

Was it different? Had it changed? Was there some trace to be found of what had happened to Sian, over and over? The Endless took such traces into itself, stretched and changed and shuffled them, but Sian's world was different. Evidence remained.

Except any evidence of Sian.

Panic scratched at her again and she remade herself to avoid its claws.

"Nothing at *all*?" Sian was saying, her voice a symphony of heat-wet-soundwaves until Trillin remembered how to hear properly. "I mean … it was hours each time. I wasn't exactly not doing stuff that wouldn't, um. I mean, sweat, right?"

Trillin had the horrible feeling she understood where Sian was going.

"If it was *all* of me coming back each time things reset, where are all the extra skin flakes and stuff going, if they're not popping back here with me? They're not back *on* me. I think. I don't feel any grubbier than I ought to be." She sniffed herself. "Possibly. I mean, it's not been the least stressful day."

Trillin was putting off making a mouth to speak with. She furled up her body: legs, torso, shoulders, mostly humanoid except for the emotions pulsing too visibly across her skin.

"Which do you think would happen first, do you think?" Sian asked, her voice hollow in the quiet Trillin's silence left all around them. "I drop dead of old age, or—"

"Stop," Trillin gasped desperately. The image was too clear in her mind: the two of them lying together the way they had been before Sian gasped and turned to her, desperation wild in her eyes. But she wouldn't turn to her. There would be no desperation in her eyes. There would be nothing.

And she wouldn't remember any of this. She wouldn't know why.

"There must be something we can do." She searched everything she was and had been. "The Endless does not understand time magic, but your world—"

"I've tried everything I can think of."

But she hadn't given up hope. Trillin searched Sian's face and body for the signs she was learning to read, and added: *yet.*

Fear flurried across her body, leaving chasms in its wake. She was glad Sian couldn't see her like this. "Does that mean there are spells to stop it, and you have tried them in – in another version of these hours?"

"More than once."

"What spells did you try?"

"It's hard to explain, but—" Sian drew a sharp breath. "Do I need to explain? You can look in my mind and see it, can't you? God, that's so much easier than trying to convince you using words. I don't know why I didn't think of it before."

"Because it is a *terrible idea*!" Trillin protested.

"No, look – you can do it, right? There are records. Well, there's one record. A survivor from the wreck of, um, a ship? I should remember the name. I might in a minute. Important thing is, she said the Endless read her mind. Turned her thoughts over in her head. And, honestly, you taking a look at my thoughts might be a good thing – a fresh pair of eyes. Or more."

"She didn't survive."

"What?"

Sian's eyebrows shot up; a sliver of eyeball appeared between her lids. Trillin surged behind her and waited, all parts of herself held carefully out of sight, as Sian swore and covered her eyes again.

"Shit. *Shit.* I forgot."

"She didn't survive," Trillin repeated, gently this time.

"No. No, you're right. I remember now. She survived the first encounter and then killed her way through to the Endless herself." She ducked her head, and Trillin caught the edge of what must be a grin of some sort, her lips peeling back from her teeth. "Hah. You don't even need to look into my head to see what I'm missing."

She took a deep breath, and Trillin knew what she was going to say even before her tongue twisted around them. "But the Endless *wanted* to destroy her. You don't want to destroy me."

"I do not know what damage I might do, even not wishing it." It wasn't enough. She needed to say more, find better arguments – surely someone, somewhere, had had this same conversation?

If they had, she didn't remember. Because if they had, they would then *not* have been devoured by the Endless, along with their memories of the conversation.

But there were oh, so many people who had tried to defeat the Endless by becoming it.

Sian licked her lips. "Destroying me would be one solution, wouldn't it? Absorb me the way the Endless absorbed all those other poor fucks. Then we could see whether only the bit of you that was me repeated back, or both of us."

"Never," Trillin swore.

And this time, she saw the stars fracture before Sian did.

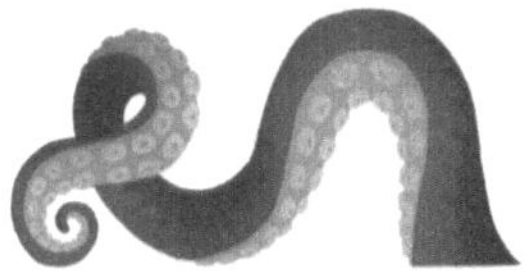

The next reset was easier.

Trillin believed her. Trillin was horrified by the evidence of the time loop, Sian changing between what seemed to her to be one moment and the next. Trillin demanded they find a way to stop it.

Like checking off boxes on a list. Tick, tick, tick.

She didn't bother bringing up the idea of having Trillin rummage around inside her to pull her thoughts straight. Her reaction the last time round made it clear that wasn't a goer. And interesting as it would be to know if the reset still affected her and only her if she was no longer the same self she'd been when this started – if she wasn't herself *alone*—

"Sian?"

Trillin looped tentacles around her arms, nudging her away from a train of thought that was in danger of becoming seriously derailed. Sian shook herself. "Yeah?"

"There is something."

Sian's chest tightened. "Something what?"

"All around you, like…"

There was still enough light that Trillin cast a shadow. She couldn't look at her directly, but how had it taken her this many repeats to realise she could see *this*: an echo of Trillin's changing body, rippling over the ragged ground. Shadow tentacles that moved like water. A floating mass that on anyone else would have been a head haloed with mermaid hair, but on Trillin, who knew?

"Like *this*," Trillin said, carefully triumphant with her pantomime shadow-play.

Sian stared. "Like … water flowing around a stone in the river?"

"This world is splitting around you, and around echoes of where you have been. But you have not been in all the places since we began talking! Not *this* time." Trillin turned, a forest bending in gale-force winds. "There – you went that way? Before?"

Sian stared where she pointed. The other direction to the spine of mountains. "Not that I remember," she said slowly. They had gone to all sorts of places, together and alone, but never back towards her home. "What is it you sense that way?"

"The same thing as here," Trillin told her, carefully, wonderingly. "This world, moving around something that is no longer there."

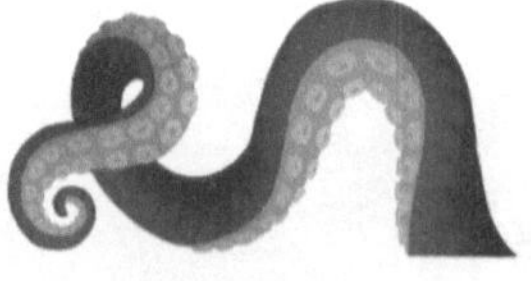

She was right. She had *helped.*

Sian had not told her how many times they had failed, but the trembling in her muscles and the strange blankness that overtook her gaze between bursts of action spoke louder than her words. They had failed, and failed, but now, Trillin had found something new.

She skeined magic through herself, ready to tear a hole in the world and pinch it together to turn the journey of a day or more into a single step.

Magic screamed all around her. She half-turned to Sian, the words already hovering in her gullet – *I did not know you could create portals, too!* – when the expression on Sian's face froze her.

Sian's panic did not appear as spikes and scales. It burnt in action. Before Trillin could speak, the transportation spell was complete. Sian ran through, pulling Trillin with her.

They arrived in a world of swirling vapour, grey in all the shades that shadows knew. Sian hissed something, her breath becoming part of the whirling, and yanked them both backwards into a place of still hard edges.

"Missed," she gasped. "Fuck. *Fuck.*"

The vapour was still there, contained behind mottled glass. Or – no. The glass – *window,* Trillin categorised it absently – contained Sian and herself and everything else within these hard edges – *walls.*

"Where are we?" she asked.

"Uni," Sian replied shortly, and then seemed to realise more words might be needed. "Uh, the university. My department. Where I study, uh, where everyone…" Her voice trailed off. "Where is everyone?"

She fell silent, and the silence all around them slid in to fill the space. No other voices, footsteps – Trillin concentrated – no damp breathing or fleshy pulse of blood hidden beneath skin.

"We are the only ones here."

"Okay, well, that's not necessarily a bad thing." Sian reached and found something that passed for Trillin's hand; she made a few adjustments, and it passed better, well enough to wrap fingers around Sian's wrist. The pulse near the joint fluttered against her touch. "One good thing about that other version of Earth, at least you could walk around with me and no one screamed their heads off."

Neither did you. Trillin seamed her mouths shut. There was so much she wanted to talk to Sian about, but this didn't seem the place for any of it. The *department* coiled crookedly around them, a hive of angled corridors and doors firmly closed over whatever lurked behind them.

"The whole place is an enchantment. I don't know if you can feel that. But if it feels a bit weird, that's probably it. Air's as nasty as ever. Stale and tingly." Sian's shoulders twitched. "Took me years to get used to it."

"What is outside the walls? Where we landed the first time?"

"Took me years to stop asking that, too." There was a frown in Sian's voice, but no time for Trillin to wonder whether that meant she should ask more or less.

Something around the next corner creaked. A fragment of conversation, and a door thudded shut.

"Someone's coming."

Without looking, Sian thrust Trillin behind herself. Trillin twisted herself small, a cramped vine of watchfulness, eyestalks sprouting tentatively to peer past Sian's legs.

The newcomer stormed around the corner. Something flitted at her ankles, and that was what Trillin saw first: a ribbon of black fur, four-legged and with gleaming orange eyes. *A cat*, she decided, which meant *not* part of the human who was making most of the noise. She looked up, past sturdy legs and a rounded midsection to a face that looked like someone pretending to be her beloved.

Sian burst out, "Flora?"

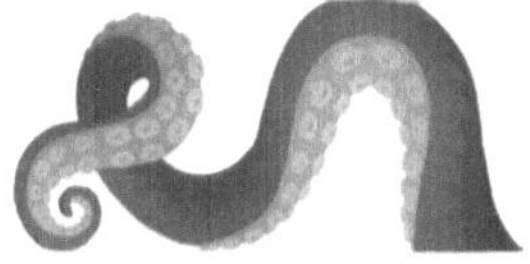

Flora stopped. She stared at Sian with wide frozen eyes. Whatever calculus she usually went with to decide whether Sian was someone she wanted to see or not seemed to have frozen, too, so Sian went first.

"I thought you were still in London. What are you doing here?"

The ice shattered. Sisterly recognition narrowed Flora's eyes. "I'm here because you're dead," she snapped. "You've been dead for six months! What are you doing here?"

"What do you mean, I'm dead?"

"Your bloody university said—"

"What do you mean, *six months*? And what does that have to do with why my un-magical sister is wandering the halls of my extremely magical university department? Did someone bring you here?"

Flora spread her arms. "You see anyone here to bring me anywhere?"

"Well, no, but—"

It couldn't be her. That was the only explanation. They'd encountered copycat aliens in that other dimension, hadn't they? And doppelgangers were rare this end of the world, but not unthinkable.

And Trillin was still hiding behind her. Even if this was her sister, she needed to – she should—

"How can you be here?" she asked. "Magic is opaque to non-witches. You don't see it, or if you do, you forget. You shouldn't be able to even find this place." She hesitated. It was the one silver lining to the way their parents had died – in a car crash, not by magical means.

It meant her sister remembered they'd existed.

Sian licked dry lips. "You should barely even notice if I'm dead."

"Well I fucking did. Do. Whatever. And I didn't want to forget, so I have magic now. That's how," Flora said thickly, the words muffled by something Sian had the horrifying suspicion might be tears.

"But how do you have magi—"

"You talk a lot for a corpse, you know that?" Flora swiped her sleeve across her face and sniffed angrily. "Except you're not dead, are you. It was just more of your magic bullshit. Well, great. Guess I'll fuck off then."

"Wait, you—" Sian took a step forward and almost tripped over something. "What's that?"

"A cat." Flora's voice could have withered whole gardens. "Don't tell me a witch can't recognise a *cat.*"

She turned and stormed back the way she came. Sian hurried after her, swerving around the cat. It darted to trip her again. She narrowed her eyes at it. It was … black. And slinky. With orange eyes that weren't familiar at all, except…

A breath rustled against her neck. There was no way Trillin would reveal enough of herself to make a mouth and all the apparatus she needed to speak normally, so the voice that shivered into her ear must have been formed some other way. She wished she could see it.

"Not a cat," Trillin breathed, and Sian had to agree. Especially as she had info Trillin didn't.

She called after Flora, "Sure looks a lot like your *ex* for a cat—"

Flora spun around. "So what if it is?" She marched towards them, rage fighting the tears in her eyes.

Shit.

"If she comes much closer she'll see you," Sian hissed under her breath.

The air behind Sian rippled. "I will hide myself," Trillin whispered with an earnestness that didn't prepare Sian for her girlfriend winnowing herself into something like a silk scarf and coiling beneath Sian's clothes.

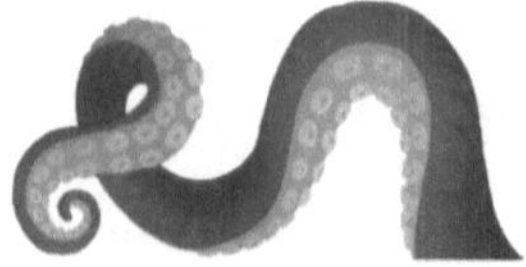

It would have been impossible to stay near Sian and keep herself hidden from the other woman. This was the perfect solution: from beneath Sian's clothes, she could keep as many stealthy eyes as needed on the other woman and the not-a-cat, without risking being seen or getting lost the way she had the last time she'd been in Sian's world.

Perhaps Sian would have difficulty with the extra weight of her body wrapped all around hers, but Trillin had thought of that; she braided tendrils around Sian's legs, twining around her joints and muscles to brace against the floor where the hems of Sian's trousers touched the flat surface.

Sian made an odd noise.

"So what if it is?" Flora snarled, poking an angry finger at Sian's face. "It's none of your business! You're *dead*, you'd been dead for half the fucking year before Aunt Helen remembered long enough to call me in tears and by the time I got here she'd forgotten and we had to do the whole conversation over again, and – and – I flew all the way back here to identify a body that wasn't even—"

"Ngk?"

"Are you even *listening* to me?"

Was Sian listening to her? There was a strange tension in her body, around which Trillin was wrapped so thoroughly that every breath and heartbeat, every hair standing on end in every follicle, every bead of sweat prickling through her pores, was echoed in Trillin's own shape.

Sian made another strange noise. Was she having trouble breathing? Trillin prodded the sensitive muscles around her ribs and she jumped.

"Yep. Listening," she blurted out, far too late even in Trillin's estimation for it to be believable. There *was* something wrong with her breathing. Concern spiked through her – and into Sian. She jumped again.

"Sorry," Trillin breathed against her skin, and Sian released a trembling breath.

Trillin paused. Every part of her stilled, and then movement began again almost of its own accord, her body exploring a concept almost entirely new to it.

Now that she thought about it, was this—

Was this…?

Flora snorted. "Okay, so, you're alive. Great. Now if you'll excuse me, I have to get back before everything goes tits up again."

"What do you mean *again* – wait, are you aware of the time loop—"

"Just stop it!" When Flora looked back this time, tears glimmered in a snaking trail across her cheeks. Sian flinched as though the sight was a physical blow, but that couldn't be possible, could it? Seeing things shouldn't hurt like that. "Come on. I *don't* want to have this conversation again."

Flora turned and stormed off. Trillin hid beneath the prickling weave of Sian's shirt, but couldn't resist sending out fine eyestalks to follow the woman and her … not-a-cat.

Sian seemed equally unable to let the conversation dissipate the way Flora wanted it to. "You're telling me you've somehow transferred Mal's magic to yourself, and he's – did *you* do that to him?"

"Do you really think that's the most important issue here?!"

"If I don't know what the issues are, how am I meant to rank them?"

"Look—" Flora's face twisted into another shape that made Sian brace herself as though for a blow. Then her mouth snapped shut. "Great. Classic Sian. Anyway, hurry the fuck up, they'll be back in a minute."

Sian gaped, and Trillin resisted the urge to curl a tendril into her mouth. "Who'll be back?"

"Everyone."

It was really bloody hard to concentrate with Trillin wrapped around her like a sensual towel.

Sian's brain misfired at the best of times. And this? Not the best of times.

"We've got to go," Flora insisted, with a hint of the whingeing Sian remembered so well. "I don't know what's going to happen if they bring you back and you're already here, but it can't be worse than anything else they've done."

"Bring me back?"

"*Hurry!*"

"But—"

Flora was already gone.

And Sian was still … *wearing* Trillin. Flora hadn't started screaming at any point, so she couldn't have seen her.

"You have any idea what's going on here?" Sian murmured, in case Flora exploded back around the corner and found her talking to herself – to her underwear – to her – her…

This was bad.

This was *so* bad.

And in any other circumstances – well, not the sort of circumstances she and Trillin tended to find themselves in, but different circumstances, quiet, private, possibly after finding out what Trillin looked like trying to drink a glass of wine, definitely not involving time loops or alternate dimensions – in *those* circumstances…

Sian swallowed. They weren't *in* those circumstances.

She needed to stop thinking about it.

Trillin peeked out, her chin resting on Sian's shoulder as she looked down the corridor where Flora and the not-a-cat had disappeared. "She thought you were dead."

"Yeah." There was a slim chance this was another thing she didn't need to think about right now, but she got the impression that way of thinking was a trap. More likely, all this was connected.

Trillin sent wandering tendrils down her arms as she wondered out loud. "She came here to discover whether that was true. And she found your colleagues *bringing you back.*"

Sian hissed in a breath that had almost nothing to do with the tendrils tickling her inner wrists. "She said 'this time'. She's aware of the time loop, too."

"Is it possible that your colleagues here—"

"Are somehow involved with chopping the timeline into little bits and stitching it back together wrong? I wouldn't put it past them."

Flora's words ran round and round in her head. *I don't want to see what happens if they bring you back when you're already here.*

She *was* already here.

And she wasn't dead.

So who – or what – were the others bringing back?

She started to run.

There was only one lab big enough for a magical working like the one she really fucking hoped wasn't going on here. Deep in the bowels of the department, a sunken amphitheatre with rows of seating that creaked if you breathed near them.

Sian was intimately familiar with it. Havers had monopolised it for the last year as they perfected the spells that led to Sian finding Trillin, and everything else that had happened since.

What *had* happened since? What had she missed here?

Other than everyone thinking she was dead.

Or – the memory of Flora's obstinately non-tearstained face punched her chest again – or everyone had pretended she was dead.

So they could go ahead with whatever this was.

"Flor—" she called as she sprinted around the corner, but she was already gone, disappeared down another empty hallway. Her footsteps echoed as she ran.

Trillin nuzzled up the side of her neck. "Where are we going?"

She thrust out an arm. "Down there—"

The stairwell yawned ahead of them. Flora was on the landing below, the bloody not-a-cat a scribble of ink at her ankles. If they got through this – *when* they got through this – she was going to give her sister hell about that. Put it in the calendar: *Why did you steal your ex-boyfriend's magic, Flor, and why turn him into a cat at the same time? Huh? Huhhhh?*

Serious, important questions, for just as soon as the rest of the world was less full of terrifying ones.

The lighting down here was never good but it was enough to see Flora's glance upward turn into a glare as she caught sight of Sian.

"Hurry up!"

She disappeared down the next turn in the stairs. Sian stumbled on the first step racing after her, her flailing hand missed the banister and—

Trillin caught her.

Wings spread out from beneath her clothes, a buoyant mass that drifted her safely to the ground. The scream of falling had caught in her throat. The scream of seeing Trillin unravel all around her turned into a squeak as they landed and Trillin hid herself again.

Sian looked down at herself, half-expecting her clothes to be torn to bits and to start screaming again at the sight of Trillin suctioned onto her. But no. Her clothes were still there. Trillin must have spun herself fine enough to fit through the threads, to … to…

"Sian?"

"Mm?"

"Did you eat anything, all those times you returned to the same time?"

"No, why?" A thought sparked. "Could that affect – I don't know, what if I came back but the food *didn't*, or what if it did, would that mean—"

"It means that you are very close to falling over." The pulsating vine around her torso that was Trillin firmed, holding her up. "You need more than magic to survive on."

"True. The last meal I had was a whole world ago." Sian made her way down the stairs, skidding her palm over the banister. Not that she was worried about losing her balance again. Just that now Trillin had mentioned it, she was ravenous, and that usually came with a helping of annoying shakiness.

By the time they reached the lab doors, they were just swinging shut behind Flora. Of course. Sian hesitated with her palm against the heavy wood.

What was waiting for them beyond?

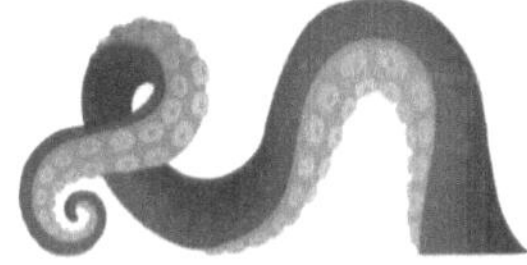

Sian's unease was so much easier to translate than the hot confusion of her skin earlier. Or – if Trillin was being honest with herself, and not carefully snipping off the budding synapse-blossoms opening into new and wonderful thoughts, and storing them away carefully for later – not easier to translate, but easier to exist with, at this moment in time, when *unease* was safer than … whatever that other thing was. Unease kept you on edge. Unease made you wary of noises and sounds and sensations. It kept you alive; it was likelier to lead to survival than … that other feeling.

They had run together through the strange building. The corridors were like a cluster of stretching empty tendrils coiling angularly through something Trillin's senses couldn't penetrate. It was like exploring some calcified being – like being her isolated self in the Endless again, but an Endless that was no longer searching, no longer alive and changing and hungering.

And now they had reached a pair of heavy doors.

"They are through there?" she asked.

"Yeah. Them and whatever they're doing here. And my sister and whatever *she's* doing here." Sian rested her palm flat against the door. It was old, and stained with the memory of a thousand other palms. And more. There were scratches and chunks taken out of it, as though more than human hands had once tried to get in, or out. All worn smooth by time.

Sian's breath gave away frustration and fear, her skin sour with it. "I know we're running out of time here. And—" She made a frustrated noise. "If they are behind the time loops, and we're close to the central working, there must be a safe zone. You'd waste time remembering what you were doing, otherwise. The reset might not hit us, if we get inside it, or might be mitigated in other ways."

Trillin waited.

"You'll remember all this." Sian's voice cracked. "At last."

"Then I will come with you."

"And you'll be in the middle of a group of witches who really, really want you dead. Probably even more than last time."

“I don’t want to lose this time with you,” Trillin insisted, and Sian let out a ragged laugh.

“You’d risk losing whatever happens next, instead? Maybe everything that happens next?”

“Yes.” She curled herself closer to the pulse in Sian’s wrist, stretched long fingers over hers pressed flat against the door. “You won’t risk it for me – so let *me* risk it for me.”

Sian’s silence was the silence of something being hidden. “Have we done *this* before?” Trillin asked. “This – this conversation, everything we’ve discovered, have you done it before?”

“No. This is the first time.” She squeezed her eyes shut, and Trillin took the opportunity to dart in front of her, taking in the twist in her not-quite-a-smile, the tension at the corners of her closed eyes. “No speed-running this one. Don’t know what comes next.”

She put her shoulder to the door and pushed it open.

Trillin peeked through her outer clothing. An empty space gulped beneath them like a stomach hollowed out, concentric circles of hard chairs staring down a central stage enclosed by a shimmering bubble.

There was so much energy bustling on that stage that for a moment it felt like the place she once called home. A dozen forms, shapeless in hooded garments that hummed and moaned with constrained magic, their movements so practised they were almost like a single organism.

Behind them, a portal so much like the one Sian first plunged through.

Sian breathed a curse. "That's—"

Not *so much like*. Exactly like. Down to the spelled rope strung tight through the portal, one end wound around a winch crackling with protective charms, the other held tight by something on the other side of the portal.

Or someone.

Flora was clutching the railing and staring down at the activity on the stage. The bubble was only an arm's length away here – one of Sian's arms, maybe. Its surface slid and glistened, but it was clear enough they could see what was happening below.

Sian sidled up to her. "Who did they send through?"

"You."

"Yeah, I mean – ages ago. Who did they send this time?"

Flora said nothing for long enough that Trillin peeked curiously out at her. Her mouth was set in an unhappy line.

Sian shuffled her feet. "How long ago did I—"

"Die?" Flora's face was stiff. "About six months. Thought I said."

"Right, so, I mean, obviously it's not me on the other end of that."

"Except you're not dead, are you?"

"Sure, but I *am* right here."

Flora breathed out hard through her nose. "I used to think it was the magic that made you hard to talk to, but I guess I was wrong about that, too."

"What?"

"Look." Flora leant forward over the railing, and Trillin stretched her eyestalks out, still out of sight, but far enough to see the strangeness in Sian's sister's eyes – the wonder and longing and dread.

The rope went slack. Sian winced, the muscles of her arms flexing in the memory of reaching and grabbing. "That'll be when I fell. The rope broke—"

"No, it didn't," Flora said absently, and then Sian stepped through the portal.

Not Sian as she was. Not Sian as she had been before Trillin turned back to her and found her changed, older, travelling a passage through time she couldn't follow.

Sian as she had been, the first time she had ever seen her, when she was still figuring out how to make her eyes see.

Except this Sian was a ghost.

"Thirty and counting!" someone called from the floor.

"Thirty what?" Sian shook her head. "Flora, you know that's not – that's not me. I never came back."

"Not until now." Flora flexed one hand, reaching out towards the shimmering bubble and then pulling her hand back. "Almost. Not yet."

"What're you doing?"

"I have to get the timing right."

Down at her feet, the little black cat let out a worried meow.

The Sian by the portal was transparent. She looked around, seeming as lost as the real one felt. She'd been smiling when she stepped back through, but now that smile faltered, its cocky generosity fading.

"Can't be real," the real Sian muttered, fingers tapping a hectic beat on the railing. "A time-ghost – but I was never *there*, so how—"

Ghost-Sian looked up at them. Her eyes widened. And as she stepped forward, arm rising to point at them, she burst into a hundred versions of herself, like a bud flowering into blossom and losing its petals all in the same instant.

They walked towards the other witches. Sprinted away, tripping over equipment that was no longer there. Sauntered with hands raised to slap against their colleagues' hands. Turned with hands on hips to peer back at the portal. Fussed with the harness that held them to the rope.

Fell to the ground.

Staggered, reaching for help.

Stepped forward and were tugged back through the portal, hands on their harnesses, shock on their faces.

But none of the other overlapped and overlapping ghosts did what this one did, staring up at them and calling for the others.

"Do you see that?" the ghostly Sian called.

The coven ignored her. She frowned, shot herself up at the railing a cocky grin, and put her fingers in her mouth to whistle. "Hey! I said—"

One of the other hooded witches looked over at her. "Ten," he said. "Nine—"

"What—" Ghost-Sian began.

"*Shit*," Real-Sian muttered.

"She's never seen me before," Flora said weakly. "I wonder if that's—"

"Four," the witch on the stage said. "Three."

"Another nothing," one of the others sighed. "You owe me ten bucks, Jonesy."

Flora bit her lip and reached for the bubble. "You only need to touch it. Come on."

And then the Endless boiled through the portal. Trillin stared horrified at everything she used to be.

Everything she would die before becoming part of again.

She shrank away, uncurling her body from around Sian's and creeping behind her, as though a single body of flesh and bone would be enough to keep her from the Endless's sights.

It would see her. It would find her, again, and make it part of itself, again, and everything she was would be it. Forever.

As soon as it had finished killing everyone here.

Flora screamed. Her cat streaked up to her face and clung, covering her eyes and mouth, but too late. The noise drew the Endless's attention. Already busy unravelling the hooded figures gathered around the portal, it spared a florid lump of itself to stretch up, up, and investigate this new treat.

The soap-bubble of magic separating them shimmered.

Flora's nerve broke. She stumbled back, tripping on the steps. Sian …

Sian wasn't screaming.

She stood with both hands planted firmly on the balustrade, staring interestedly at the monster bearing down on them.

Trillin wrapped a coiling tendril around her ankle. The muscles there were so tight they might snap, and of course Sian was terrified, of *course* she was, she had to be, she couldn't even look at Trillin without screaming, so the only reason she wasn't screaming now must have been that she was too broken even to force air out of her lungs, but – but—

It didn't matter. She needed to get her out of here. But she could not convince any part of her body to move, except for that one, helpless tendril around Sian's ankle.

Far below, the Endless was finished with the coven. It stretched into their bodies, puppeting them as it made what they were part of what it was. There was always this liminal stage, before the edges between the two beings collapsed and two became many and one.

The things that once were human raised their heads. Hoods fell back to reveal eyes pulsing with strange light.

Sian was still staring at the part of it closest to them, her brow furrowed, her lips slightly parted.

"Huh," she said.

Beneath them, as the end of the world played out within a soap-bubble of captured time, the counting witch intoned, "TWO."

"It's going to reset," Sian gasped. "Catch me!"

"What do you—"

Sian grabbed Flora and threw herself over the railing, into the bubble.

Into the Endless.

She couldn't stop them. She was too slow. Too paralysed, too still and terrified a thing to stop her world from ending.

Massy limbs tore loose from the bulk forcing its way through the portal, reaching, grasping.

Deep within her, too many other minds remembered trying and failing to save their loved ones from the same fate, only to join them when the Endless took them too. Together and eternally separate; dead grief pulled and picked over by a being that could never understand it.

But she did. Trillin did. She had made herself into something that could lose everything.

And suddenly she could move again. Could do nothing but move. She soared after Sian and Flora, into the greedy maw of her old self, tentacles whipping out to grab them and pull them to safety.

It was as useless a last stand as all the others she remembered.

But if Sian died, she would die too.

The body in her arms was warm and familiar, softness over taut muscles and hot-wet bones. Her face found Sian's neck; her hands spread over the rough pelt of her hair, her shoulders, the slopes of her hips and lower back.

An awful part of her, new-born and unwanted, thought:

If I must become part of the Endless again, at least we will both *be part of it. If I escape it again, some part of the me that escapes will be some part of her—*

"ONE," said the puppet witch.

And then time stopped.

Unwound.

The world sucked away like the tide and, when it came back, it brought them with it.

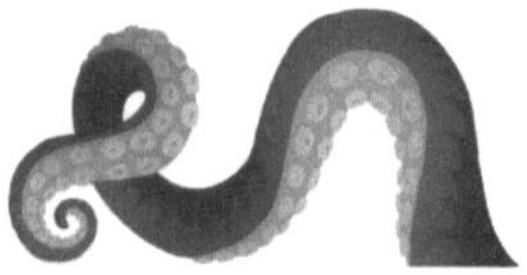

The floor rose up to greet her with a slap that took the air from her lungs, but, you know, she hadn't been devoured by the Endless. You had to count your wins where you got them.

Sian pushed herself up, muscles screaming.

"That's five breaches out of the last seven repeats," someone called, a note of complaint in their voice.

"What was the damage this time?"

Someone inspected a readout. Bloody lab hoods, Sian thought.

Can't tell who's who underneath them.

But it felt like everyone was here.

"Twelve for twelve," the witch who'd counted down until the reset said gloomily. "Not even you escaped this time."

"And I was so heroic the last time!" The hooded figure gave a dramatic shrug. "And all for what? Wasted!"

Sian's jaw hurt.

But not from screaming.

She massaged it as she rose, taking in everything all around. The rest of the coven were back where they'd been before the last repeat turned to shit. Flora was groaning on the floor with the cat.

And Trillin was behind her and all around her, slithering feather-light beneath her clothes again. Sian leant back, resting her weight against a form that strengthened to hold her.

The other witches were still hood-up, head-down in their grimoires and ticker-tape printouts. Sian turned her head the slightest amount, not wanting to catch sight of anything that would make her scream.

"Sorry," she whispered. "Didn't really explain that before I jumped in, did I?"

The silence before Trillin answered clawed at her chest.

"You did not," Trillin said at last.

"That bubble is a shield for the time resets. Did you hear them counting down? They knew time was going to run out and they would repeat – and it worked!" She laughed out loud, relief and excitement fizzing in her veins. "You can remember! You – you do remember?"

"I do."

"It worked – we're both here, we both remember, we didn't reset back to that bloody hill and—"

"The Endless was inside the bubble spell as well."

"Yes! And did you see—"

"Hey!" one of the witches shouted.

"Ah, fuck," Sian said. Not quietly. Admittedly, after reminding herself to be quiet and not draw attention while she was talking to Trillin, she had … yelled a bit, maybe.

But what she'd seen …

"Trillin, we—"

"HEY! How did you—" The hooded figure swore. "Sian? Oh god, Sian! H-how did you – Professor!"

Jonesy. Sian's heart made a semi-unpleasant thump. *Not dead.* Professor Havers – okay, yeah, she recognised him now, hunched and sniffing derisively under his lab hood.

The last time she'd seen them they'd been on the other side of a death-dealing spell meant to scour all trace of Trillin and anyone else caught in its orbit from all existence. Including themselves.

"Hey, Jonesy," she called weakly. "How's it going?"

"You're alive!"

"Same to you." She waited for Trillin to hide herself under her clothes again – no time to get distracted by it now, save it for when they weren't around people who wanted her girlfriend dead – and then sauntered forwards, hands in pockets and only slightly so no one would see them shaking. "Thought that death spell you cast last time I saw you would have killed you."

Jonesy pushed his hood back off his face. His eyes were bright. Not the creepy sort of illuminated-from-within brightness they'd been before time reset. Normal brightness. A bit sweaty.

"Something siphoned off the power. I thought that was you! The portal appeared and sucked all the magic into it – and then it was gone, and so were you. And the monster," he added after a half-beat, as though he'd forgotten the reason they were casting death spells in the first place.

Trillin tensed around Sian's ribs. The *monster*.

"How'd all this start, then?" She waved at the everything.

"Oh!" He blinked rapidly. "It's interesting you should ask that!"

"It's *interesting* I should ask why I come back here to find you all looping through time and bringing the Endless back in after you just tried to kill yourselves getting rid of it?"

"Th-that was months ago! And with the time loops it doesn't – it all goes away again! We don't even need to build up power for it – it just *goes*, and we can try something else."

"Are you sure about it *all* going?" she asked, remembering what she'd seen before time reset.

"Of course!" Confidence sweated from every one of Jonesy's pores.

"But – hmm. It's all around *you* – the you that left – but if you're back now, then – Professor, what do you think?"

"About what?" Havers sniffed.

"Sian being here."

"Don't be stupid, boy, we're not recalling the ghost until—"

"I mean she's right here, Professor!"

Havers looked up from his workings. His hood slipped enough that Sian could see his eyes widen – and the moment his surprise narrowed into suspicion.

And opportunity.

He stalked towards them.

"What the *fuck* is going on?" Flora complained, standing up at last. The bloody not-a-cat wound around her feet, whining like it was dinnertime. If she hadn't already pegged the moggy for Mal bloody Ashwick, that would have done it.

Sian raised an eyebrow at Havers. "You all know that time isn't only looping here in your working, right? It's affecting the whole world? Multiple worlds?"

"*Is* it?" Havers tapped one finger against his chin as he stopped in front of them. "Or is it only affecting you?"

"It—"

"Professor!"

Magic warbled through the air. Sian felt sick. Something tightened, twisted – and above them, the bubble fractured.

Havers hissed a breath. "Positions!"

Sian lunged forwards to help, and he shoved her back. "*Not* you," he snarled. "Find the weakness! If the shield falls before the next repeat—"

"Just stop the repeats?" Sian suggested.

"It's not that, um – it isn't that simple—" Jonesy babbled as Havers shot him an angry look.

"Get to your place, Mr Jones!"

Sian bounced on her heels as she watched the coven unite in spellcasting. She recognised the working – sort of. Bits of it, anyway. Protection, escape, revolution, circuitousness – were they serious? The time bubble *reinforced* the time repeats? But if that was right, then…

It would keep going. Forever. Whatever they'd started this for, even if they found it, they couldn't finish.

Her chest hollowed out. She began to whisper to Trillin, "Okay, maybe being in here is not the best thing in the world after all," and her sister heard her.

Flora frowned. "Who're you talking to?"

"How'd you figure out that getting into the bubble protected you from the time resets?" When asked a question, always interrupt with one of your own.

"You don't have to throw yourself inside it! You only need to touch it!"

"Meow!"

"Yeah, I know, okay?"

Trillin pressed a tendril into Sian's palm. She squeezed it. "Try to get out of here while they aren't looking," Sian murmured.

A whisper, pressed against the bones of her chest: "What about you?"

"I'll tell you when I figure it out." Sian's eyes shivered towards the empty portal, where the ghost-her had hopped so jauntily through, moments before the very real Endless followed.

There was no tight cable stretched through the portal now. It was still coiled around the winch, a few metres from the portal.

Jonesy said it was all around *her.* She'd been aware of the time loops even before she saw the working here. And what was that ghost? An echo dragged through time, or something even more fucked up?

She looked up. The bubble was rippling and boiling, its surface pock-marked one minute, stretched and splitting the next.

"It's not working!" someone cried out.

"You'd better go quickly," she muttered to Trillin, and swallowed as Trillin eased away from her.

"I'll stay within the bubble," was the last thing Trillin whispered before she was too far away to hear.

Sian didn't risk looking backwards to see where she was hiding. Not yet. She'd been able to look at the Endless – but, if she was right, then whatever had changed there hadn't changed for Trillin.

Not yet.

Not in this reality.

Flora knelt to pick up the not-a-cat and straightened. "What was that thing that came through the portal after the ghosty version of you?" she asked, shooting a nervous look at the empty gateway.

"The Endless," Sian said promptly. "An alien entity that both inhabits and is an alternate dimension, wants to devour everything it sees, ideally us."

"Oh, god, I wish I hadn't asked." Flora winced. "Will it come back?"

"Depends."

"Also not the answer I wanted."

"It's not here now. The bubble must protect anyone inside it from anything that happens before the timeline resets, but still allows them to remember – wait. Wait. That doesn't make sense. *We're* still here. If it protects everything inside – Trillin!" she shouted as the containment bubble simmered and seethed overhead. "It's still here! The Endless—"

A strong hand gripped her arm. "Clever." She looked into his eyes and tugged her arm free – fucking Havers, the only muscles he had were the ones he used to write letters of complaint – but he dragged her with a strength that wasn't human at all.

The Endless was still there. The way it had been there through how many repeats already, learning each time how best to turn this situation into a feast.

"But you can't get out either, can you?" she babbled, planting her feet. "You're stuck here with the rest of them."

The ground rippled beneath her, flicking her off balance.

"Not yet," said the thing that was wearing Havers. "But let it never be said I gave up an opportunity to *experiment.*"

Light flared at the corner of her eye, but before she could register what it was, she saw it close up. The portal.

Havers threw her to the Endless.

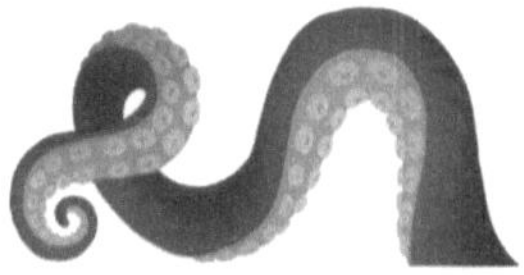

Sian disappeared through the disc of light.

And then the Endless turned its human puppet to face Trillin. It made a smile on its face.

"Come out now," it said in the human's voice. "We have a lot to learn from you, as well."

It reached out to her – hungry, *ravenous*, a light in its eyes and a twitching want in its fingers that was the last thing so many of her memories had ever seen.

The cycle had only just reset. Sian was gone, but if she moved quickly, she could follow her through the portal.

And find Sian before the Endless noticed her.

She became a cloud of dust on the wind and the wind itself, winnowing dancing between grasping fingers, between cracking bones and flesh as the Endless broke its new body into something that could catch her. The portal's hum thrummed through her, bright-edged and satisfied, and whatever was through it wouldn't be Sian, but would be all that was left of her.

As the first outstretched molecules of her touched it, the world cracked open above her. Stone and plaster, spell and wood, and somewhere far above the sky, splintering to nothing.

No, she thought, *it isn't time—*

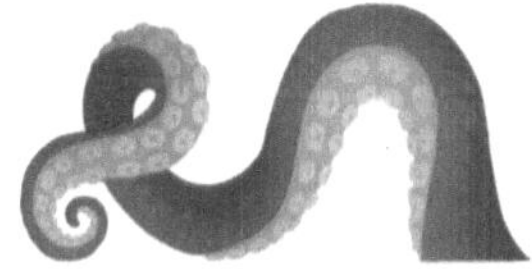

Sian was standing in front of her as the other witches got into position. She flinched, drawing in breath like she thought she would never breathe again.

Trillin flinched, too, every edge spiralling inward.

Then Sian turned, laughter lighting her eyes as she looked just away from where Trillin was and said, "Well, that didn't work out quite how I'd—"

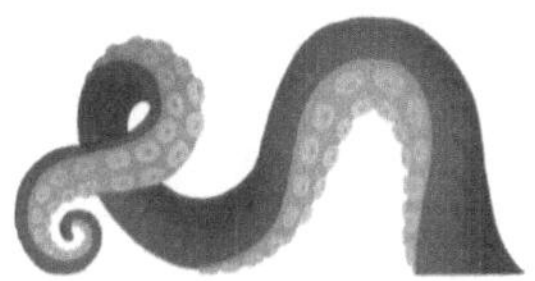

Sian was standing in front of her – but that tableau lasted barely a second before she spun around.

And squeezed her eyes and mouth shut over a scream.

"Shit," she gasped as Trillin wound steadying tendrils around her. "Okay, so it hasn't happened yet—"

"What hasn't happened?"

Behind them, Flora screamed, and—

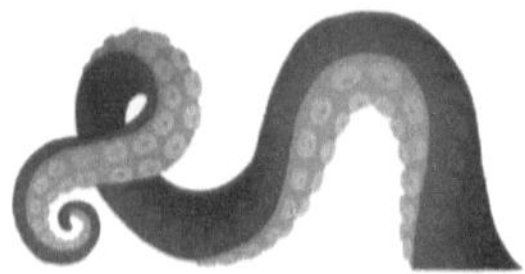

Sian threw herself backwards into Trillin's arms.

"No time to explain," she gasped, and—

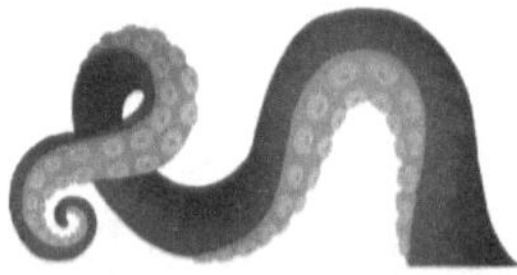

Trillin threw herself forwards, catching Sian before she could lunge towards her.

"Something's wrong," they both said at once.

"It's happening faster," Trillin quailed.

"But we can both still remember." Sian pressed her face into a crook of Trillin's body. "If we can—"

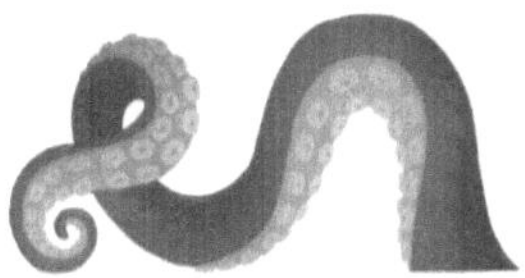

Trillin reached for Sian, and did not realise what was wrong until her tendrils began to sink into Sian's skin.

She was trapped. Absorbed and absorbing. And Sian turned burning eyes on her – she remembered to turn her neck to do it, though there was a strange crack, at the end – and smiled, open and joyous.

"This time!" she exclaimed. "It worked, this time!"

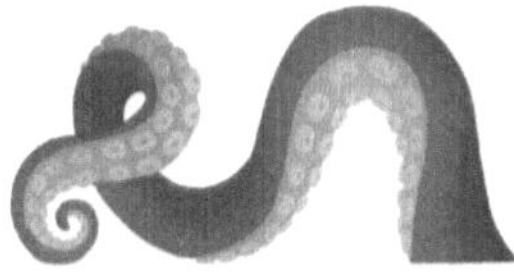

She ran from the thing Sian once was.

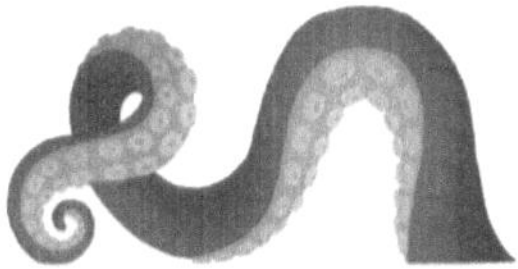

She embraced it.

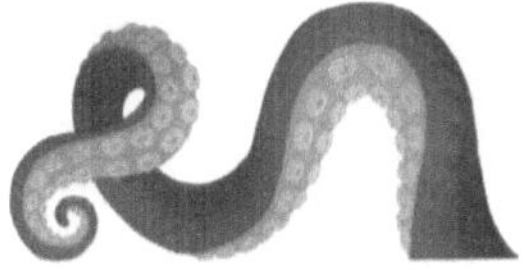

Trillin only had lungs if she wanted them; they were inessential to her continued existence. But as she fell to the ground, all herself and only herself, her sides ballooned as she gulped air.

Eyes popped open on all sides of her body, on the flesh stretched thin around pockets of oxygen it did not, after all, need; she grew claws and teeth, and coiling arms.

Sian wasn't there.

Anything Sian might have turned into wasn't there, either.

Trillin went still. And from across a room that had never been this empty, all the times she'd returned to it, Flora scrubbed at her face and stared at her hands like she'd never seen them before.

"Did you—" she said, before realising there was nobody to say it to.

Nobody except the monster who'd been left behind when her sister disappeared.

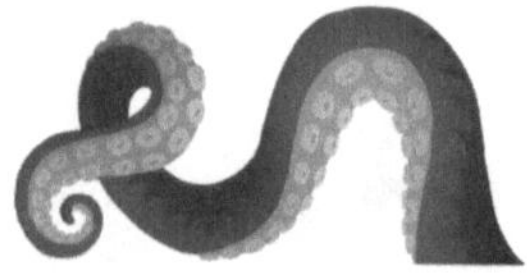

Three more repeats, to get to her and stop the screaming.

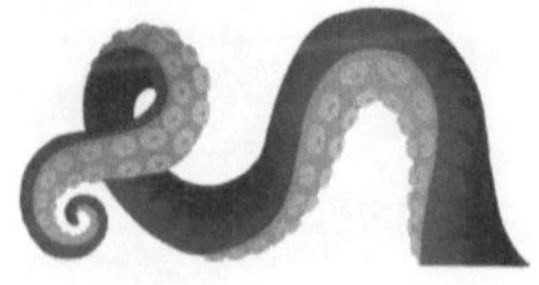

Three more, and Flora knew not to look at her.

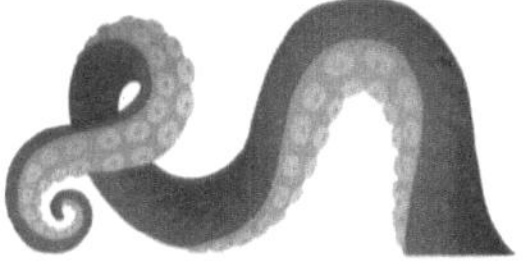

She could not risk making a heart for herself; the beating would pull her to pieces. Flora raised her hands, twining magic with a hesitancy so unlike Sian's belligerent optimism but somehow so much like her at the same time. The cat watched her, human panic behind its flickering whiskers.

And something they had both missed all those other times rose up behind her.

"Look out!" Trillin called, and something ate her words out of the air before they reached her.

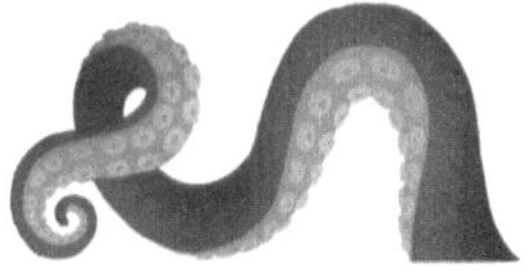

It was difficult to be surprised when Flora raised eyes like holes in the sun to greet her.

And the cat was gone.

She didn't want to think about that.

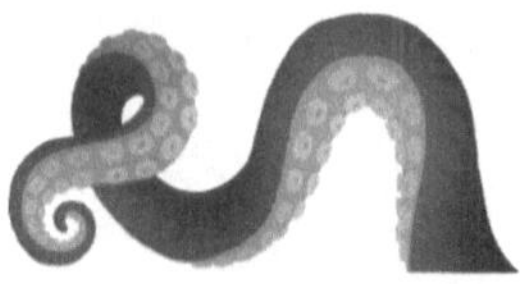

Something had changed, she told herself in the fragmenting moments she still had a self to tell. These weren't *repeats.* Something changed within each one – something had *already* changed. She was coming back partway through all the new versions of time, each time. She was forgetting—

The world solidified around her in a way that told her this was Sian's world, still. Behind her, someone spoke in a voice she almost knew.

"There you are!"

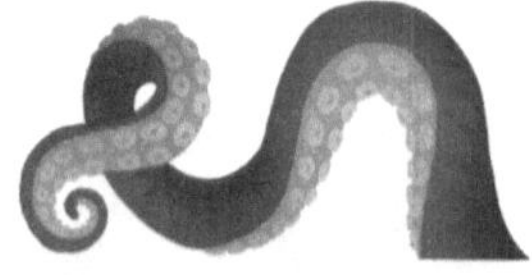

The portal spat Sian into a world that was horrifyingly familiar.

She rose slowly. No spellsuit to protect her from the Endless this time.

No safety rope harnessing her to home.

The portal was still there. She extended one finger, poking it as carefully as she could with the world rolling like a ship beneath and all around her. If she was building any sort of plan around shoving someone into a portal over and over again, she'd make sure to – yep. There it was. Pain seared through her and when she pulled her finger back, the tip was burnt red.

All right.

She drew in a breath, uncomfortably aware that what she'd thought of as oxygen last time was probably full of microdroplets of Endless. It hadn't affected her last time, but last time – spellsuit, harness, et cetera. And she hadn't known, then, and knowing changed things, she was sure someone had some sort of theory about that, so maybe she just had to hope that the potentially existent microdroplets counted as fragments, the way Trillin had started off as a fragment, and it had to be too much to ask that they would stay nestling in her lungs and not try to absorb or be absorbed by her own flesh, but that was fine, okay, all she had to do was find a way out of here before they made their way back out of her lungs or wherever else they ended up inside her and rejoined the rest of the Endless—

The world lurched. Matted flesh squelched tight and shrugged her off, so fast she barely had time to think she might die before she had to admit she hadn't. The Endless had burped her away from the portal, like a horse flicking its tail at a bug bite.

Which meant it hadn't really noticed her. Not yet. It would have done a hell of a lot more than flick her off if it had. And the thoughtless flick had done more than dislodge her from the fleshy land around the portal. It shook her brain back into shape. Her thoughts, which had been in danger of spiralling in a thousand useless directions, found the right track again.

She had to get the fuck out of here.

Whatever was lurking in her lungs and anywhere else could wait.

But – a single thought strayed from the pack – if she could figure out what had happened, to the Endless or humanity or some combination of the two, which meant she'd been able to stare at the Endless and Endless-inhabited coven back at the department without screaming bloody murder, then … that might be worth the delay.

The air thickened around her.

Or she might die.

Which was probably one possible route to what she'd seen—

Run, the final remaining sensible part of herself groaned, *for the love of whatever god might be paying attention.*

She ran.

Three years of failing to map the Endless had taught her how pointless it was to navigate in the ever-changing. Trillin had known her way around her old existence's twists and turns. When they'd been here last, Sian had fallen…

…There.

She looked down, and saw her own footsteps racing ahead. They didn't move. They were the one thing in the Endless not moving.

She remembered what Trillin had said: that Sian's aura was like a stone with the river parting either side of it, and she'd felt the same thing in the coven's department beneath the university.

Footsteps like stones, and the Endless surging all around.

She shivered.

How many times had her ghost walked this path? If she followed it, would she find the same escape path she and Trillin had taken the first time, or…

She frowned, and looked closer.

That was the tread of her work boots. The scuffs at the toes. But there was something else. The tracks seemed calcified, somehow, as though they weren't just unchanged but had hardened the world around them to keep themselves unchanged.

Or the world around them had hardened itself, to keep them.

A trap.

Huh.

Did that mean the Endless was already aware of her being here? Was this all some sort of game?

But the Endless didn't play games.

Her skin prickled all over. Still squatting in front of the footprints, she looked up without moving her head. The Endless showed no sign it had noticed her. Shaggy cliffs stretched up and joined with rib-like extrusions beneath a boiling skin of sky. On what passed for the ground, the landscape shifted as though it could not decide between being gravel and green-tinted growth. Lumps moved beneath the surface, bubbling closer and drifting away.

Sian's heart raced. Trillin had made herself from *this.*

...which it must have figured out, by now.

She rose slowly.

Right on time, part of the Endless sloughed off from the main, unfolding delicate limbs and a face that was – that was...

"You won't remember, but we already did something like this," she said out loud. "Twice. There were those copycat creatures on that one world, and—"

"How can you think I am a copy?"

Her voice sent shivers across Sian's skin. "And the whole Evil Queen business."

"I remember."

"No, you can't remember, because—"

"I do! I was there!"

"You weren't—" Sian broke off.

The Endless hadn't been there. Trillin was separate from it; it couldn't share her memories the way it shared the memories of everything that became it.

But time had been repeating. Untidily enough that she could remember each repeat, and each relived handful of hours had made its mark on her. What if the same were true of the Endless? That must be how it had made itself into something that didn't cause madness when she looked at it on her Earth.

But if it remembered everything?

"I *was* there." Mouths broke out in smiles all over the fragment's face and chest.

Well.

Fuck.

"Good to know," she forced out, words dry as her throat. "How'd that happen, exactly?"

"*You* don't remember?"

Don't get caught up, Sian told herself desperately. It's intriguing. Course it fucking is. Intersection of your study of the Endless and this new time bullshit and everything Trillin is – everything the two of us could be, together…

"*Sian.*" It couldn't be her Trillin, but her voice was fond and exasperated and something new, something her Trillin had never yet been. Or had she? The repeats were muddying in her head.

There had to be another way out.

"Sian!"

Urgent this time. Tendrils whipped in something like a panic, tearing free of and sinking back into the cliffs behind her. And above and all around them, the Endless writhed.

Sian looked up.

There was no sky to splinter here. The Endless itself cracked apart, instead.

And wove itself over the splintered pieces. The Endless surged up to repair the holes in its fabric, dragging the thing that remembered being Trillin with it. Displeasure made thorns on her body and she pulled herself free.

A separate thing, new-made.

Sian grabbed for handholds as the ground bucked and twisted, but couldn't drag her eyes away from the new fragment. The creature shrieked with triumph. She made and remade herself, exulting in her self, and Sian saw—

—Echoes.

The river breaking around a stone that was no longer there.

Sian threw herself at the path before she saw where it led – not back to the beginning, not out into the far reaches of this or any other universe, but sideways.

Splintering.

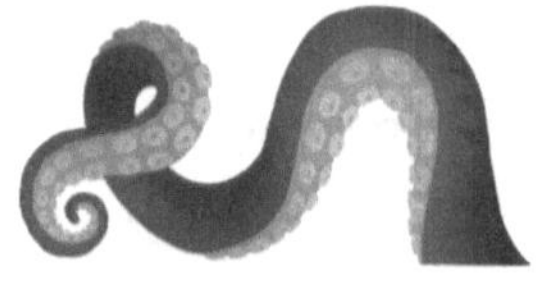

She hung in the outbreath of an explosion, every broken piece of it trapped unmoving around her. She wasn't a stone with the river parting around her anymore, if she ever had been; she was soft and gasping breathless, surrounded by possibilities like shards of glass bursting out from a collapsing core. She could move and break them; she could move and they would break her.

She didn't dare breathe.

Okay.

Think.

First: the coven had done some time shit, using her foray into the Endless as a … centring point? Spindle? They could wind time out from there, and then wind it back in. But not well enough that shit hadn't all gone to fuck, a description she would have to rethink if she ever found herself in a position to report on this properly.

Second: the Endless had used the repeating time loops to … do something. Become something more than it already was. Which was kind of its deal already, but it had never done *this* before.

She'd stared at the Endless on Earth and not lost her entire goddamned mind.

Whatever else ended up happening here, wherever and whenever *here* was, she had to figure out how to take that change and make it work with Trillin.

What number was she up to now?

Fourth (possibly): she'd ended up in this broken lightbulb of a sideways world way, wayyyy too early in the current time loop.

She was going to be stuck here for *hours.*

Not daring to breathe because the shards might – okay, so, maybe she could try to breathe a tiiiny bit…

And when breathing didn't kill her or shatter this world any more than it already was, she lifted a hand – carefully – and poked one of the glittering shards.

Her finger went through it. Into it. She wasn't bleeding, at least? Her finger and the shard were still both there, and then—

"Ouch!"

She yanked back her finger and the rest of her jerked back, too, scything through broken glass that wasn't glass, the sheen of light on something that didn't exist.

One struck her eye.

She blinked. The blink dislodged it, somehow, so when she opened her eye again she was staring into another world at an angle that made her head spin. It was – It was *her*.

Staring straight back at her, face wrinkling wryly, mouth opening and shaping words with no sound.

Something stretched long suckered fingers around her neck, eyestalks popping like blisters from wet knuckles, and Sian barely had time to think *Trillin!* before terror bloomed hot in the dark of her mind.

And then she was back in the flowering explosion of glass.

Forget not breathing. Forget anything but breathing, for now at least, ragged wet sobs that stuck around in her body even after her mind twigged to what was going on.

When time had looped before, she'd found Trillin.

She'd never found herself before.

Something had changed. This was new. Which meant waiting around for the reset might mean waiting around for something that would never come, here in this … wherever she was…

Her eyes narrowed.

Her finger still hurt. Carefully, she moved it where she could see it, and the line of puncture wounds where something had bitten her. Something like a cat, maybe. Or like and unlike a cat.

And in the other one, she'd seen herself and Trillin.

What was this? Not a loop anymore, but – getting here had felt like moving crabwise, not back and around again.

If her own world was still caught in a loop, maybe what she'd seen was where those loops ended up.

And if she was going to find her way home again – *Trillin,* she thought again desperately, and with a similar but more sinking desperation, *Flora and that fucking cat and Aunt Helen and Jonesy and Havers and everyone else, oh god…*

She winced until the panic receded.

She *was* going to find her way back home again.

One of these shards had to be *her* world.

She reached out more carefully this time, feeling through the gaps between shards to determine that, yes, they might look a finger's-width thick from here in the middle of the explosion but from around the side they were more like panes of glass than slivers, and fell through.

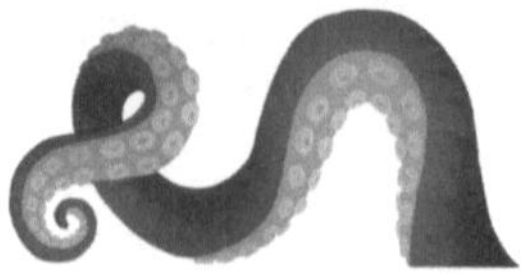

She found herself again first. What was left of her. A scream that ended a moment before she got there. A body that wasn't, anymore, or not much of one anyway.

Her stomach – her own one, the one still inside her – lurched, and she threw herself further down the splintering path.

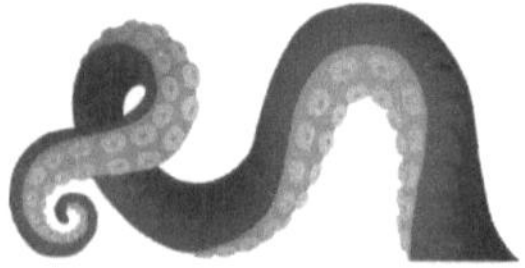

Trillin lost bone, lost ligaments and muscle and cartilage and the feathery mass she had no name for; she fell into shapelessness, everything she was skittering mercurially away from the touch of something that would make her everything she did not want to be.

The Endless's touch was a physical thing, the stuff that had been not-Sian's fingers digging in. It was already becoming her. Glimpses of memories that weren't the ones she'd brought with her from the Endless, or made herself since then.

She scoured herself away from them, losing slivers of herself in her haste to be only herself.

Heat flashed. Her outer parts sizzled, senses burnt away so quickly pain was a thud of should-have-been, not something she actually *felt.*

"All done!" a voice cried brightly. Trillin didn't have ears, but the soundwaves found her, and her body translated them automatically. She dragged herself into a shape to see and hear.

And looked up.

Into her own eyes.

"Don't worry!" she told herself, flittering nerves over a rolling throb of sincerity. "I know you must have seen so many different versions of this – of us – but don't panic. Nobody here will hurt you."

Eyes – *her* eyes – so many of them – coursed up and down her body, taking her in. She echoed the gesture.

"What is happening?" she asked weakly, in a voice that sounded so different from within her own body, than hearing it from the outside. "You are—"

"We are both Trillin. Because of the alternate realities. Time itself, splitting and remaking itself. You must have figured that much out, at least?" Curiosity quested luminescent and grasping from eyes so like the ones she made for herself. "And you are afraid, because every other version of reality you have seen until now has been … not good."

"I saw—" Her throat vanished before she could say more.

"I can guess. But don't worry." A grin flashed over the many mouths on this other Trillin, starting at the one closest to her and twisting wryly as they got further away. "You don't have to worry about that here. We are the original world. And everything here is going to be just fine."

It got easier, falling through worlds, and in a minute she was going to start suspecting that was a bad thing.

When she found Trillin again, it was the wrong Trillin.

Sian stared up at a creature more human than any of her own species, and infinitely wrong. It bent reality around it. A second ago, a world ago, Sian never would have said that being human meant having that many gaping maws, or jagged-clawed limbs, but this Trillin *was human, was everything humanity was.*

It had Trillin's eyes.

And Jonesy's.

And Bunny's. But they'd left Bunny in that other world, how could she – and—

An insectoid limb reached for her, the serrated claw melting to something feather-light and so soft she didn't realise until it tilted her chin up that it was even touching her.

Her Trillin never felt like that. When she touched, she wanted Sian to know she was touching.

Wrongness curdled in the back of Sian's throat.

"The wrong one again," Not-Trillin said in a human voice from a human mouth. She tilted Sian's head this way and that. "Again! I'm sick of seeing my reflection in the wrong people's eyes."

Sian jerked away, backing into a barrier she didn't notice until she stopped moving. It wasn't just the texture she'd made unnoticeable, she thought, wrenching a foot loose and finding it held fast in another soft barricade. It was the temperature. Perfectly regulated to human skin. Like how you couldn't feel *wet*; you could just feel the hot or the cold of the water.

You could feel skin. Skin was a thing you could feel even if it was skin-temperature. What would be the point, otherwise?

But human skin had stuff behind it. Weight. Mass. Fat and flesh and bone, and organs, and stuff. It didn't map itself so precisely to you that you couldn't feel it until you did something it didn't want you to do.

This creature was everything Trillin was, and nothing she was.

"I'm in a shit tonne of trouble, aren't I?" Sian said out loud.

"And here I thought you weren't listening to a word I said." A beautiful, human smile.

Fuck fuck fuck fuck fuck, Sian thought, managing to keep it inside her head this time.

"You're not even screaming." Not-Trillin paused, considering. "Mine doesn't, either. Though she's gotten better at listening."

Not-Trillin. Was her Trillin meeting a not-Sian, wherever she was?

"Or perhaps not."

"Wait. You've seen other versions of me? Of us?" Maybe there was a way to backwards-engineer the splintering timelines. Back-navigate them. If she could find the splitting point, and … do something…

"There's no going back. That's what caused all this excitement in the first place." Not-Trillin flexed her segmented human arms.

Too late, Sian saw the other arms Not-Trillin had crept behind her.

As they closed in, something lunged out of the darkness and tackled her. Magic burnt, a portal the shape of a person blistering outwards as it was made to fit two instead of only one, and a new world closed around her.

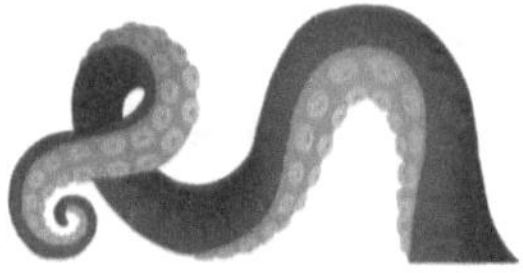

"This is the original timeline?"

Trillin was finding it a struggle to speak as she normally would. The brighter the other Trillin shone, the weaker she felt. The more energy pulsed through her tendrils and behind the living orbs of her eyes, the more she pulled in her own tattered edges.

"It is," the other Trillin said earnestly. "Which must be a relief, after what you have seen." Her too many, too beautiful eyes saw too much. "How many times did it get through?"

She did not need to ask what *it* was. "The Endless was already there by the time we arrived. It came through, but it had left fragments of itself in previous loops, as well. Don't – don't you remember that?"

Her extremities twitched with suspicion.

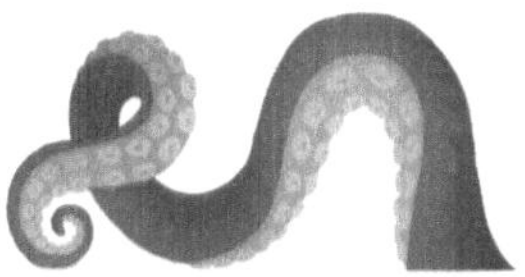

Sian stared into her own eyes.

Human eyes. Actual human, not … whatever Not-Trillin had been.

She wet her lips. "Have I turned up in front of a mirror this time, or—"

"No," the other her said. "No, and – don't look around. You don't want to see it. Trust me." She barked laughter that sounded strange coming from outside Sian's own body, but maybe it would have sounded strange anyway. Bitter and manic. "Listen. I made a list."

"You what?" Sian leant closer and grabbed the apparition by the arm. By her arm. Fuck, this was weird. "Okay, so, you're one of those copy-cats from that first world we visited—"

"I thought that for a bit, too. Would have made it easier, right? No. No copycat versions of us. Just *us*, every time. But listen. You're still trying to work it out, aren't you? It's only been—"

Eyes too much like her own searched hers.

"Look at you," Other-Sian half-smiled, her voice cracking. "Still looking wonderful."

"What are you—"

"Still figuring it out. Right. Me too. But I can tell you what it isn't." Other-Sian flipped through a ragged notebook, using her fingers as bookmarks while she found the page she was after. The same way Sian always did, despite the fact she'd be lucky if she even remembered what she was holding the pages for by the time she got back to them. "The Endless isn't a far-future Earth, where our devouring magic has devoured everything until there was only ourselves to devour. It isn't our past, either."

"Why would it be our past?"

"You've seen it already, haven't you? Have you? There are so many other Earths but *no other Endlesses.* I know the time splintering stuff makes it confusing, but stick with me. The reason our dimensions are so much a part of one another. The way our magic makes us want to go there. Where it all started. *How* it all started. I think it was us, somehow, but I don't know *how.*"

"Why does it matter?"

Other-Sian stared at her with wild eyes. "It has to matter. It—" She gestured around herself, then grabbed Sian's chin and forced her to look at herself before she could look around. "It *has to matter* because there's nothing else left *to* matter and if it doesn't matter then – then—"

Her voice cracked in a way Sian's never had.

All those worlds, and this was the only world she'd found where she had been left alone.

Growing up a witch meant knowing the magic would get you eventually. You were going to die, the only question was how explosively.

You were the one who left. Not the one who was left behind.

The other Sian heaved in the sort of breath Sian did when she'd forgotten to breathe for a while. She flipped to another. "We thought destroying it would help. Spoiler alert. It doesn't. Don't do that."

"Destroy what?"

"The Endless."

"How can—"

"Just don't do it, okay?" The other Sian wasn't looking at her anymore; she was looking past her, through her. At something that hurt. "It could be worse, right? Gotta believe that. It could be worse."

Sian thought of all the other worlds she'd seen. "Could be," she agreed.

"Liar. But listen. Whatever the answer is, it won't matter if you don't have time to find it. And the only way to have time is to find her." Grief streaked across the other Sian's face, and she felt the twitch of it echoed on her own. "Us finding each other started this, in every version of the worlds in which the two of us exist. And the only versions of those worlds that *still* exist are the ones where we're both still there. In some form or another. No matter how fucking grim the rest of it gets."

"Is that a good thing?"

Her eyes darted in a way she'd never seen from the other side before. "It's a thing."

"But *you're* still here."

"Yeah." Her lips peeled back. "Had a look outside recently, though? I'm not sure I'd call this existing."

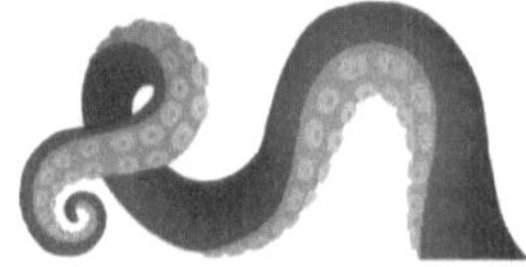

She repeated, as much to drag the memories into order in her own mind as for the shining Trillin's benefit: "The Endless was here before us, every time. It learnt from what it watched the coven do. Learnt from their minds when it devoured them, and learnt another version of them when time reset and it watched them again. You *must* remember that."

Trillin blinked in surprise. "Of course I do not remember! I told you. This universe is the original. Everything you've seen, and your own world – they all sprang from us. Like…" A dozen eyes shone. "Like when I first made myself. Do you remember?"

She remembered. She thought she was the only one who *could* remember.

"This is wrong," Trillin forced out.

"I know it must feel that way. Believe me. So many of you have felt the same."

"How many of us have you met?"

"Of myself?" Trillin's attention seemed to waver. "Many."

Many. Many versions of herself – other sprouts from this universe, this Trillin, this *original.* Who had carried on, secure and self-contained, as all the while Trillin thought herself unique.

The feeling that stabbed through her was strange and sharp, and made her want to curl into herself.

She had thought herself the only fragment to ever make herself – but she was only one of many.

Shouldn't that be a good thing? Part of her wondered, and the answering thought shocked her.

No! So many of us, with all the Endless's knowledge, all the potential to be like it – what if one of us DID become another Endless? I can control my own edges but I can't control so many pieces outside myself!

It wasn't a new thought.

It was old. So old it had forgotten it was a thought at all; an ancient, ossified pearl, churning in the Endless's depths.

The shock punched emptiness through her. She hurried to fill it before the other Trillin saw.

But something told her this Trillin, who'd already met so many of herself, already knew what she was feeling.

The other leant closer, a thousand eyes endlessly eloquent. "Tell me about what you have seen. What you have experienced. It may help us figure out where things went so wrong in so many worlds. How many other realms did you visit before you returned to your Sian's Earth?"

Trillin's attention swarmed at her. "The realms we visited together, or the places I have been since then?"

"Together."

She had nothing to be suspicious about. Nothing that was not part of herself – and she was more suspicious of *that* than ever. So she told her.

The copycats who'd made such easy game of taking her and Sian's forms – her tendrils twisted, remembering her reaction to that, and her reaction to this other Trillin now.

The little pocket of no-worlds that had kept them safe, the two of them and Bunny, until it was destroyed.

The dragon that had destroyed it. The strange magic of this other version of their world, split off by magical catastrophe years before she or Sian had existed.

Uncertainty crinkled along her inner scaffolding. "But if that happened long before our timeline split, then—"

"This Bunny. You never devoured it?"

"No!"

"Oh…"

The other Trillin's attention drifted. Her body drifted, too, unspooling on invisible waves as she processed this information. "Or any part of this other Earth? This … earlier version of our world?"

"No. The magic changed me, but I changed myself back. I got rid of it. I am only myself."

Whatever that was.

The other Trillin lapsed into thoughtful loops again, and she pried at the thought that had twisted into a knot during their conversation. The fairytale-bespelled Earth had split off from Sian's Earth many years ago – or had it not? Had it split off from this original Earth, and then her and her Sian's worlds were an even later outcropping?

Why did that feel so much lesser, when she already knew she was only a fragment?

"Another world that split before all this." Trillin sounded excited. "And you cannot be the only other version of us to have survived this. All those fractured realities. Some of them might still be saved."

"But if you're the original—"

Something strangely familiar twisted Trillin's face. "We're the original, so that means we shouldn't bother trying to save as many other versions of ourselves as we can? We should sit and *wait*, like that ever helped before? We just waited until it was too late—"

"Until what was too late?"

She waited, but the other Trillin was silent.

"You said the Endless never came through, in your world. So what *did* happen?"

"Everything fell apart. If I had acted sooner – if I'd come back here as soon as I understood—"

"My Sian and I came back as soon as we could, and it was already too late."

"And you saw – what did you see? How was it different to the other places you've seen? There must be a way out of this."

"Out of what?"

"Out of—" Trillin wavered. Her fretful expression melted; something else rose up in its place, tearing free the way Trillin herself had torn free of the Endless, the way they all must have.

But more violent.

More desperate.

"It didn't work!" cried the fragment that was more Trillin than the whole it had pulled itself loose from. "Don't listen – it didn't work, it *won't* work, tell her I'm so sorry—"

And then it was gone, devoured by the whole.

Who was Trillin … and more than Trillin.

Trillin's senses chimed a warning. "But you said the Sian here—"

The other laughed, dry and hacking.

"You said she was *busy*," Trillin said, hoping that she didn't understand; that this was all a mistake.

"Pretty bloody busy, yeah," Trillin said in her lover's voice.

She edged away. The other didn't stop her, and she followed the so-straight edges, the impermeable solidity of this world. Everything as she remembered it.

But it wasn't her memories she was moving through. And it wasn't her mind that held this world together. Trillin knew how hinges worked; she had learnt it patiently.

Whoever had made this world had not had to learn hinges as carefully as she did. And the edges of things, the details, were slapdash, except where they were bursting with sudden attentive detail.

She did not have a heart to sink. She did not let one form, did not even build protective ribs around where one might be. If she was afraid, she was afraid for her own Sian, lost in some other world, not what she was looking for here.

She couldn't be far away.

She found her slumped against a wall. Not part of the wall, though now that she knew what she was looking for, she saw it was all part of her. The wall. The university.

The other Trillin.

It wasn't the Endless that devoured everything in this world.

"Sian?"

"Ah," Sian murmured. "Here's the brave knight."

Trillin lowered herself near her. "The part of you that is me said you never went to that other world," she said softly.

"No, but we've heard enough about it. I have. We … does it still count as there being two of us?" She saw something in Trillin's gaze and grimaced. "No. I didn't think so."

"What happened?"

"What seems to always happen. No matter what world it happens in. Shit went wrong, and we couldn't fix it."

"But if this is the original—"

"I hope to fuck it isn't. But everything we've – I've – found out from you lot who keep popping in…"

"How did you find it out?"

"By asking?" She gave a weak grin. "Eventually. Once I figured out how not to…"

Perhaps she did not need to make herself a heart for it to hurt. "How not to devour everything you wanted."

"Yeah."

"I'm sorry."

"You're sorry?"

"You got that hunger from me. From the Endless."

Sian laughed wetly. "No. Oh no. The hunger is all mine. The ability – you can take credit for that, sure. But not the hunger. That's always been there."

Even in her own Sian, wherever she was? Trillin thought.

"Tried to keep them all separate," Sian was saying. "But it's too difficult. How do you manage it?"

"I don't."

"But that means – but if you're right, then Trillin, my Trillin—"

Sian's voice and face cracked.

Trillin held onto what she could, fighting her own instincts to keep from absorbing this Sian and all her pain. "She must have told you, before you did this."

"She knew. I hoped … I hoped she was wrong. I wanted—" She squeezed her eyes shut and growled, "I *still* want. There must be some way to fix this. To fix it *all*. For everyone—"

She gritted her teeth. They cracked and fell inward, and grew back again. "You found a world with no Endless at all. We can start there. They must have what we need."

Sian was right, and wrong. Some of the hunger might have been her own. But Trillin knew this one.

"I do not think that is true."

"Their alternative timeline split off from ours far enough ago that everything that happened since I went through that portal won't matter. Trillin and I don't even exist there – that's what the other one said. She didn't know how to make the portal that took you there, but *you…*"

She looked up, and her face went slack. "I could kill you, couldn't I, and find out? That might fix everything."

"I expect not."

"You wouldn't." A crooked smile that might have been all that was left of the Sian she knew. "You'd better go quickly. I'm not good at changing my mind, once I hit on an idea. Never have been."

"How do I go?"

Sian tilted her head back, interest bright and clear in her eyes. "Funny you should ask," she said. "I have a few theories. Either it's something to do with—"

Light flared beside Trillin, and the world splintered open. Sian fell against her.

Not the Sian slumped against the wall, bones caving in on themselves as she forgot to hold them up. Her Sian. Alive and warm and—

"Something to do with *me*," the Sian on the floor gasped, and all the world reached for them.

Her Sian dragged her away.

To a place that was strange and familiar, cold and warm, bright and so dark it hurt everywhere it touched.

A place that was already dead and had never lived.

They hung in what must be air, because Sian was breathing it. Below, the ground was cracked and hazy with dust. The same black dust outlined the ghosts of faraway hills.

This was where they had landed after she rescued Sian from her happily-ever-after in the other world.

"Is this our world?" she asked, horrified.

Sian laughed against her, face buried in warm and welcoming skin. "No. It's somewhere that hasn't happened yet."

"What does that mean?"

"The instant before an instant. The time waiting in the wings to exist. Probably not a thing that's meant to exist, let alone as a place, but I guess the universe got sick of me crashing through walls and put me in here to calm down."

"Did it work?"

"I made it out to find you, didn't I? And made it back again. We're still falling, did you notice? Slowly. And when we land … I think it's our own world waiting in the next moment for us. I hope it is. I was beginning to think it didn't exist anymore."

Trillin paused, hunting through herself for the right thing to say. Hunting past all the ragged edges where something else had been.

Something else that might have known something *better* to say.

"Long day?" she said at last.

"Has it only been a day?"

"You've seen terrible things."

"Seen terrible things. Been terrible things." Her voice was flat, like it didn't mean anything; then it cracked, because it did.

"I know."

Sian lifted her head, and Trillin had never regretted learning more of her lover's expressions until now. Her eyes were screwed closed, and the irises jerked behind the lids, trying to see. Or escape. "I think we did this, Trillin. I think we broke everything."

"I don't think…"

"What else can it be? In a thousand worlds, a thousand versions of us found each other. And where are those worlds now? Gone. Dead or dying."

"Maybe not all of them—"

"Did you see any versions of this where things had gone *well*?" Sian growled and twisted away. "It's us."

Trillin tugged at her chin until she looked up at her, and that bitterness cracked to show the desperation beneath. Still with her eyes shut, because even here in the instant before the world started again, Sian could not look at her.

"The other you thought that, too. But you're both wrong. You want it to be your own fault so much, but whatever happened here started long before either of us. Long before what either of us is now." Uncertainty coiled through her. "But it is something between our worlds."

"Only our worlds. Not Victor's world, where the death wish used up all the magic. And so many of those other dimensions we visited when – before – when time was repeating." Sian swore. "I almost lost track of that. All the realities where shit went wrong were versions of our own worlds. Everything's wrong, but it's only wrong *here.* My Earth, and your Endless, over and over. Why here and nowhere else? Does the Endless not exist in Victor's world?"

"If it did, nobody there was looking for it."

"Here, we barely look for anything else." Sian sucked breath through her teeth. "When did that start?"

"I cannot remember." Frustration whipped through her. "I should be able to remember which came first! If there are worlds in which it *didn't* happen, then it is clear something must have happened, but I cannot remember it!"

She looked down at herself, at the still-ragged edges where she excised every bit of the Endless in every world that tried to make their way into her.

"Perhaps it rid itself of the memories," she wondered out loud. "After … whatever happened."

She remembered the hunger in the other Sian's eyes. A hunger she knew from her own Sian's delight to discover more of each world they found; a hunger she felt the echoes of deep inside herself.

"I think—"

She hesitated again. It hardly seemed possible, that she should be able to think up a thing that no version of herself or anyone else had thought before.

"What is it?"

Trillin wisped uncertainty, and Sian wrapped one arm around her.

"Come on, out with it," she urged her. "If anyone can think us up a way out of this, it's you."

How could she trust her so completely? Trillin didn't even trust herself that much.

And she certainly didn't trust what her theory might mean.

"What the Endless eats, it becomes, in part. It is everything it devours. It uses their memories to learn, their knowledge to know more. It is too large for most of their feelings, though, because it already feels so much—"

"Hunger," Sian breathed. "And if we're always hungry to find it, too … We feed the cycle by being fed on. But where did it start? Or if it started long enough ago, when did it *stop* for Victor's world but keep going for ours?"

"I think we used to be together." The words came out piecemeal, a syllable here, a breathy cluster of sounds there, all her mouths unsure how to speak them all at once. "One thing. The Endless and your world. That – that we were the same, or close enough to that it made no difference. That's why the Endless wants your world so much. It wants you back, the same way it wants back every fragment of itself that ever broke free. But it doesn't remember *why*. I can make myself forget things, by getting rid of the piece of myself that holds those memories. If the Endless shed the part of itself that remembered—"

"Or the part that remembered left, taking the memory with it." Sian's gaze went bright and distant, her lower lip trapped between her teeth. "Could a fragment of it do that? Pull together *all* its memories of something and take them out with it? … Trillin?"

Trillin shivered, pulling herself out of the spell cast by Sian's teeth holding her lip so gently between them; gnawing, rolling back and forth, but not tearing and devouring. "I did it. I took everything that was me, so it wouldn't know how I became. I thought – I thought I must have been the first…"

Her voice trailed away as her mind wound through the possibilities, and it took another nudge from Sian to remind her to keep speaking out loud where she could hear her.

"The only way I knew I had succeeded was that it did not notice me leave. That was the only reassurance that I had taken my memories with me, not only a copy. If another fragment had done the same, long before … Of course the Endless would not remember. *I* would not remember."

"The Endless didn't find you, because you'd taken its memories of where you meant to go," Sian breathed. "But – if that earlier fragment found humanity and became us, or whatever happened, then *we* must have forgotten, too. Because we kept wanting to go back, and why would we if we knew—"

"You must have lost it, as well. Excised the knowledge from yourself."

Sian wrinkled her nose. "No need. We don't pass on memories like that. It would become history. Stories. Nothing."

"But it – I – *we* do. And you were part of us."

"Until we weren't," Sian said, her voice a veil of smoke over deeper thoughts. "Is this what it was all about, then? Some part of humanity, or only the part of humanity that's magic, or maybe the Endless became our magic, somehow – always wanting to find the piece of ourselves we cut ourselves away from. The Endless always wanting what it had lost, even if neither it nor we can remember. And then when we finally find what we were looking for, we can't bear it, seeing what we once were—"

She broke off suddenly.

"So that's what went wrong." All over her body, Sian's muscles tightened beneath pebbling skin. "For hundreds of years, we've existed in this cycle that feeds itself. Hungering and eating the hunger. And then the two broken halves found each other again."

"Humanity has encountered the Endless before."

"Not like this. Whatever we were looking for in all those other worlds – whatever our own magic was hunting for when it sent us towards you, hunting and hungry…" Her palm was warm against Trillin's cheek. "I've found it."

"But so did all the other versions of us."

"Nah. Just us. We were all the same one of us, then. It's only since we met that things started to splinter." Her smile was crooked and too unhappy to be truly happy – but too happy to be truly unhappy, at the same time. Trillin had never seen it before. "In all possible worlds, all possible versions of me choose you. But they chose other things, too, and the choices they made weren't the choices *we* made. For the first time, the Endless touched a human, and didn't devour it. And I touched you, and wasn't destroyed. All those centuries our two worlds had been feeding on one another, consuming and consumed. A cycle that dug itself into the flesh and magic of both worlds. What happens when a cycle like that breaks?"

"Everything broke," Trillin whispered.

"Like some sort of machine that works perfectly until a single weakness develops, and then the whole thing shatters. We met. You didn't eat me, I didn't worm my way into you and change who you were from the inside. We chose differently. And every time my bloody coven used that moment to power their time magic experiment, it broke things more." She grimaced. "All the other versions of us I met split off before we got back to the university. Was it the same for you?"

"Yes! They never left your Earth. Or they returned earlier – or to a different place—"

"Or ate Bunny. And everyone else. Or died."

"I doubt that was a choice they made deliberately," Trillin pointed out with hesitation.

"I don't know. Remember how I tried to save you last time?"

"I wouldn't let you."

"Maybe you didn't always get to decide that." Her face tightened. "Maybe I didn't, either."

"And each new ending—"

No, they hadn't all been endings. Each new path taken had taken away from the cycle that had told their world what it was for hundreds of years, until the centre could not hold. And all those wandering pathways had shattered, shattering each other in turn until she and

Sian returned, and the splintering caught up with them.

"We're the last ones," Trillin whispered.

"We're the end of our world," Sian agreed. "And all it took was a kiss."

"More than a kiss."

"I thought you didn't remember that time?" Sian sank against her. "That's our world through there, you know. An instant away. An instant that's almost here."

"How can you tell?" Trillin wondered.

Sian grimaced. "I'm the one holding it off. Hey. Do you think some version of us will splinter off and get another chance to do things over, if we stuff this one up?"

Trillin hesitated.

They had both seen the ends of so many worlds. And she had seen more – all the places the Endless had found in its search to feed its all-consuming hunger. All the places that would never exist again, no matter how this world ended.

"Does it matter?"

"S'pose not. Not like we'll be around to not-enjoy it."

"I do not care if some other version of us does this over. I care about *this* version of us. You and me. And I care about *this world*."

In no memory the Endless had ever stolen from humanity had kissing your beloved in the face of disaster staved off certain doom. But she kissed Sian now, desperate and longing, as though a kiss could change anything.

She surrounded Sian, touching every inch of her and casting the touch into a memory nothing could ever take from her. Sian returned her kiss, her lips as hot as the need that seared through parts of Trillin that had never known what to exist for until now. She *wanted.*

She *hungered.*

Trillin tore herself away. Sian grabbed hold of her. She could easily have escaped her grasp – exploded into ribbons, vanished like mist.

Instead she slumped into Sian's embrace.

"I'm sorry," she whispered.

"Sorry you almost ate me up?" There was a strange rumble in Sian's voicc. "You know you wouldn't have."

"No, I don't!"

"Fine. *I* know you wouldn't have."

"I wanted—"

"Even if you wanted it." Sian pressed a chaste kiss to a tentacle. "You never freaked out like this when we kissed before, so let me guess. You saw another version of yourself who took me over?"

Tendrils furled and unfurled, clutching at nothing. "There was still enough of her left to regret it," Trillin admitted.

Sian let out a huff of mirthless laughter. "How'd I end up?"

"*She* ended up mostly *you*. And you hated it."

"I would. Fuck. Poor them." Sian rested her forehead against her again. "But, Trillin – I don't know her. I know *you.* I know you're so wary of where you end and the rest of existence starts, you wouldn't do anything like that by accident." She raised her head, and her eyeballs moved behind their lids, as though she was trying to see what Trillin wasn't saying. "And I know I'd have to convince you to do it on purpose."

"We – we've talked about this before?"

"Once. That was enough." Her lips curved into a smile that invited touch, but – Trillin wished she could look into her eyes. Sian was hiding something, but her eyes were always honest. "But, hey. If you're worried about kissing me, and both of us are happy ignoring the fact we're one moment away from the end of the world? I can kiss you instead."

"Please."

Sian's eyes were closed. Trillin kept hers open as Sian lifted both hands to cup a face she made to fill them; she watched, breathless even though she didn't need breath, more curious eyes blossoming over every other part of her, as Sian drew her close and pressed her lips against Trillin's skin. Slowly. Tenderly. The rough edges of her thumbs teasing new textures from Trillin's outer dermis, her breath warm and damp, each touch slow and deliberate and giving.

Even after everything she must have seen in all those different versions of them, she wasn't afraid. And with every breath she spent on her skin, she took away Trillin's fear, too.

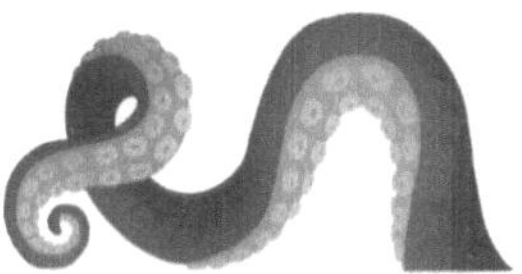

It started slowly. Trillin held herself more still for Sian's kisses than she'd ever known her to be. Then the body in Sian's arms burst into massless ribbons and swirled back together, whirling around itself as though it didn't know whether it was trying to escape or embrace the emotions burning through it.

Trillin was all joy – and Sian gritted her teeth, because what she was about to say next was not what Trillin wanted to hear.

"Can you do something for me, now?"

"What do you want?" Even her voice was honeycombed with delight.

Sian swallowed. "I can't keep us here much longer. We're going to end up back in my world. I need you to figure out what the rest of the Endless already did." She took a deep breath. "Look inside me, and find what makes humanity fear you so much. And take it away."

Trillin turned to ice. "No."

"We're going to get there and the rest of the Endless will already know how to do it, Trill. And I won't even be able to glance at you out of the corner of my eye without turning into a sitting duck." She kissed her again, an apology and a plea. "It figured it out by killing my coven over and over. If anyone can figure it out without doing that – it's you."

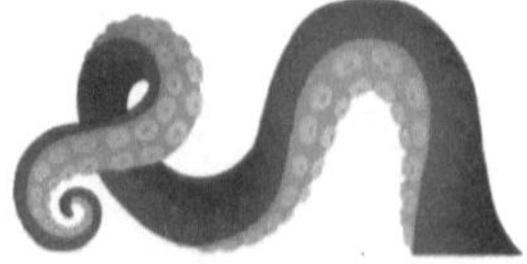

"No!" Trillin repeated. She billowed away from Sian, not letting her go in case letting her go meant falling out of this pocket out-of-time, but not letting any part of her drift close enough that they might combine. As though Sian was the danger here, and not her. "How can you ask me that?"

"It was a shit move, I know, kissing you and then landing an idea like this on you, but—"

"I won't do it!"

"But it might be the only chance we have to—"

"You can't ask me to do that! You're reckless, and you won't let anything stop you, Sian, and I love that about you, but you can't ask me to pull apart what you are!" Horror spiked along her edges, repelling, defensive. Terrified. "What if I broke you?"

"You wouldn't—"

"I did! I have! So many of me!"

"You're not like them!"

"What makes me anything else? They made themselves. I made myself. They are *me*, all the choices and memories I made and took, and—" She couldn't say it. The words stopped. Her mouths buried themselves deep within her.

Sian was relentless. "You said it. Part of the Endless must have once come to my world. That's what makes us different from the worlds where I could look at you without screaming. The Endless is always the Endless but the humans in that different Earth must have been *different humans.* Whatever we did to ourselves here to make us notice the Endless in our world and shriek like a fire alarm, if you can find it and get rid of it—"

"I don't want to get rid of any part of you!"

"And I want to see you before the world ends!"

She opened her eyes.

Trillin wheeled away, but Sian held her tight. Water beaded on the skin around her eyes and her grip began to shake.

"If there's only one thing we fix I want it to be this," she choked out. Her face mottled, grey and purple. Colours it shouldn't be.

"Stop it!"

"I won't – I *want you,* I want us to—"

"No!"

Whatever Sian had been doing to hold them in the moment before the world, her control broke. The world rushed in all around and had always been there.

The long, scratching grass. The dry crumbling dirt. The distant hills, and the sun a kiss on the horizon.

Sian groaned. She'd stumbled back as her feet hit the ground and time hit her, and was leaning over with her hands covering her face. Trillin ventured closer to her. "Sian?"

Sian swore. Profusely. At length. And still didn't look up at her. Which was a good thing, wasn't it? Sian's body had almost shattered under the pressure of perceiving Trillin; she shouldn't have even tried.

But – she wanted. And Trillin wanted, too.

So much it frightened her.

"Right," Sian said at last. She gave a weak laugh that Trillin half-wished fooled her, but didn't. She knew her human too well to fall for it. "That's enough. You're right. No reckless rushing in. Stupid. Okay."

"Are you—"

"I'm fine." Sian straightened, sucking in air through her nostrils, one muscular forearm still over her eyes. "Where are we? Back where we started?"

"Yes."

"Your first time, or—"

"Second."

"That's something, at least." Her arm dropped, and she stared into the distance. "We've got a few hours, then. Options."

She stopped. Licked her lips.

"Except we've already seen how so many of those options end up, haven't we? Stay here. Try to escape. Go back to the university—"

"Your sister will be there," Trillin said, and it might have been the worst thing to say.

Sian's mouth twisted. "I know."

"So is—"

"I *know.*" Her eyes went strangely blank. Not the blankness of terror. Something worse. "She survived how many repeats before we showed up? And then I..."

Her fists clenched. "It's not meant to *be* like this," she whispered savagely. "I'm meant to disappear someday and she never knows why or, or even notices! She's not meant to see that I'm gone. She's not meant to be magic, too. Because if she is then there's no escape. Even if we get through this. Anything magic touches always ends up the same way. How can I protect her from that?"

Trillin had never seen her so hopeless. She had never known her Sian to be so full of hollows. Depths that pulled down into darkness. "Do you mean, your magic here—"

"What've we got? A few hours? And saving the world's not even the half of what we need to do with it." She barked laughter – still not convincing, but a different type of lie – and straightened her shoulders. "Fuck it. Might as well try, right?"

Trillin was preparing to nod when the earth trembled.

She whipped out a defensive fence of tentacles around them both. Sian tensed, flinching away from the sight.

Above them, the sky tore open.

And the Endless flooded in.

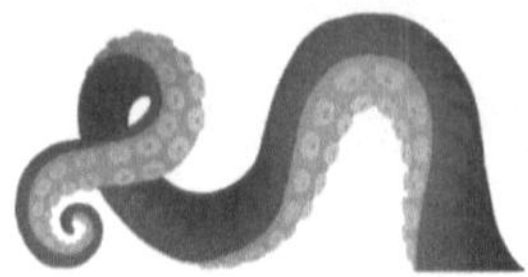

Certain death was no time for uncertainty.

As Sian stared upward at the fleshy tentacles bursting from the cracks in the sky, she was certain of one thing.

"It did it," she breathed, as the Endless boiled its victory above the world. "All those repeats, all those times the trapped fragment of the Endless hid in the containment spell and devoured each new thing the coven learnt … it learnt how to exist here without us being paralysed with terror. And it let itself be eaten up by the rest of the Endless again, to teach it how to do it."

It occurred to her she should probably be afraid anyway. Not the mindless fear of her human mind disintegrating as it tried to perceive the unthinkable. Normal fear. The creature crawling out of a hundred cracks in the sky wasn't inconceivable, but it was still going to kill them all.

That sort of fear.

"It's here," she said instead, and something in her was … *happy.*

She licked her lips.

Was this what that eldritch terror had hidden all along?

"Stop looking at it!" Trillin suggested, a hint of outrage in her voice. "We can still get away."

"I think you were right." It would be the easiest thing in the world to look away, but she didn't. Not yet. "It's like magnets."

"Magnets? Sian, what are you talking about?"

"We thought the fear was something the Endless did to us. A trap to hold us in place. But this is … I could move, if I wanted."

"Do you want to?"

"I don't … know…" She grinned at the sky. "Isn't that weird? And incredible? Why would the Endless take away our fear of it if it was going to attack openly like this? I thought it must want to stay secret, to hide – but this – how does it benefit? Does it change something about us, about what it can take from us? Do *we* benefit?"

"You can *move,*" Trillin insisted.

"True, that's better than being frozen in terror – I could move if I want to now – but why—" Her brain was on fire, thoughts splitting off in a thousand directions as the sky boiled above. "Maybe *we* made the fear, or whatever is left in us that remembers we don't want to get eaten up again, and the fact that the fear was so great was a mistake – we wanted to stop ourselves being enraptured by it but we just made a different sort of trap – so—"

"So let us *not get eaten up again*, Sian!"

She blinked. "Oh. Right." *Focus,* she told herself, *focus focus focus.* "Can you stop me looking at it?"

A tentacle folded over her eyes, and her diaphragm cramped on a scream until tiny tendrils peeled her eyelids shut.

"Ta."

Deep breaths. Trillin's words lingered in her mind. *Don't be so reckless.* She wasn't the first to say something like that. Nobody who knew her really had much patience for her tendency to throw herself into things headfirst. Unless they used it to their own advantage. How much of the glee in Havers' eyes at finding her back in the lab had been the Endless looking out through him, and how much had been him?

File that under *thoughts that aren't actually that helpful right now, thanks anyway.*

"It hasn't seen us yet," Trillin said. "The centre of the fracture is far away, the same direction you took us in last time."

Back home. Her heart bucked in her chest.

She was building the portal before she knew what was happening. Her fingers scoured magic from the air, shaping it to match her intent.

And then the magic poured out of her grasp, coiling out into the dusk like water seeping into the sand. She swore.

"Someone else is calling the magic to them," Trillin marvelled. "All of it."

"They're casting something that big?" She swore. "But that will kill us! Maybe not now, but if they use all the magic for this—"

They would end up like the fairy tale world, all the planet's power bound up in a single enchantment. Or worse. That enchantment had been a wish that repeated itself – if this spell was just to destroy the

Endless, then what would happen when it did its job?

"There is no way that ends up that's good," Sian gasped. "Either it destroys the Endless entirely and uses up all the magic in the world and we all die of magical dehydration, or—"

"Or it destroys everything. It finds everything that ever was the Endless, and kills it, too. Including you." Trillin's voice was suspiciously distant. "Oh, Sian, my witch. I wish there was a point to saying I wish we had more time together. But time has not been our friend, recently."

Slowly, strand by strand, Trillin pulled away from her.

Sian clutched blindly for her. "What are you doing?"

There was a fleshy thud nearby, in the space where Trillin wasn't answering her question.

"What was that?"

Trillin's voice was a whisper at the end of the world. "It has found us."

"But—"

"Don't worry."

The tentacle over Sian's eyes slipped away. She twisted after it, reaching, and fell to her knees with empty arms. "Where are you?"

"I never wanted to go home again," Trillin whispered. Another thud.

"Then don't. Whatever you're doing, stop it. If the Endless has found us we'll fight it together."

She opened her eyes, staring wildly around. It was dark enough that any of the shadows around her could have been Trillin, but none of them were.

And the massive tentacles driving themselves into the earth all around were the wrong sort of terrifying.

Trillin's voice wafted down from above.

"This is not the end. I promise you that. But if whatever comes out of there is not me … be kind to them?"

Sian stared at her. Terror clawed up her oesophagus. It dug deep between her ribs, a fishhook in her guts holding her in place. "No."

"Please."

She would not scream. She was so afraid. "You can't—"

"If I don't, you will," she said. "And I can't have that."

Sian's mouth was still twisting around another *No!* when Trillin threw herself into the abyss above the world.

The Endless … stopped.

Time didn't. The sun still sank down behind the horizon, somehow, even with all the holes in the sky. But the huge limbs of flesh bursting through those holes were frozen.

Long enough for Sian to start breathing again, after Trillin disappeared into them.

"Wait," she croaked, stupidly, and far too late. "You can't …"

Nobody heard.

The fighting stopped, too. The death spell that would have been the death of them all lost sight of its prey, and lost its shape. Was the Endless no longer enough the Endless for the spell to recognise it?

Sian tried to think what that meant – tried to give her mind something to latch onto, a problem or a discovery to obsess over – but it didn't help.

Her world's magic gave one great pulse and sank back into the landscape, breathing itself back into the air. The Endless was no longer a threat.

Whatever Trillin had done, had worked.

She'd saved the world.

And left Sian behind.

She watched until there was no light left, and then she cast an illumination. Magic responded the way it always had, with a shiver of conspiracy. The hanging lights moved on the breeze, making the trunks of flesh seem like they were moving.

So when they did start moving again, she almost missed it.

The Endless changed. It was slow, and liquid, a sheen of coagulating fat that drew the eye away from what was happening beneath, until the frozen mass of flesh was all – was all…

"Trillin?"

Blossoms and filaments, cilia and blooming algal growths. Scales like little moons. Eyes like galaxies, and mouths like the welcoming sea.

It *looked* like Trillin.

And this must have been her plan. Not to let herself be devoured by the Endless, but to devour it. To make every bit of it a bit of *her*. The person who'd made herself. Who'd been so careful and curious and loving, sweet and gentle like she'd come up with the concepts herself, because how could they have existed in the thing she came from?

She'd been so small. The Endless was vast. But she had changed it.

Into what? Sian wondered, hope a hook in her chest, and crept closer.

Her heart sank. There was no fear. No devouring terror.

And no want, either. This Endless that Trillin had changed to make it become herself – she felt nothing for it. Nothing but the hope that she would feel *something*.

And the feeling of that hope being dashed.

From the first time she'd caught sight of the fragment of the Endless that watched her back, there'd been *something*. The tingle of initial interest. The wonder that filled her mind and thrilled through her blood: *Could you feel that way? For a fragment of the ENDLESS?* The reckless excitement of Trillin joining her. The breathless heat when she figured out Trillin was as interested in Sian as Sian was her.

The way each patchwork emotion had grown, stitching themselves more elaborately together. Head, heart and lower regions, all working together. For the first time in Sian's life, a relationship that didn't burn hot and fast and then cold just as quickly. The real thing, she'd figured.

Love.

And now it was gone.

The cold that had held tight to her skin dug deeper as night fell. She should have seen this coming, shouldn't she? Anyone else would have. Classic Sian. Banging her way through the local demographic until anyone else would have headed overseas to refresh the dating pool, but she hadn't even considered leaving.

Because that would have meant abandoning her guaranteed access to the Endless.

And now look at her. Guaranteed access an arm's length away and she didn't give a shit about it being the Endless and didn't want it even though it was all there was left of Trillin, her Trillin, who had given everything she was to shape the Endless around herself and now—

Faces appeared in the nearest fleshy trunk. Sian stared, stomach not just sinking now but curdling, too, as the outcrop of the Endless tried on a dozen familiar shapes. Faces Trillin had worked so hard perfecting.

Be kind to them, Trillin had said.

Oh god.

She stepped forward. Scattered eyes stared at her in confusion. Recognition washed over them in uncertain waves. She lifted a hand.

"Hi," she said, weakly, unable to muster the energy to even fake a smile. "You did it. You saved the world. My world, I mean. And you…"

Her breath caught. "Trillin?"

Not the eyes and scales and fluttering skeins of tendrils. Something else. She stepped closer, calling light to her hand to see better.

"Sian," a dozen voices murmured, none of them Trillin's, and the Endless reached for her.

Not, in any version of reality, a good thing. Trillin had given herself to the Endless, but Sian still had no way of knowing what the Endless had made of that gift. It was so vast, and Trillin was so small, and it wasn't like she actually knew why the distant witches had stopped fighting, was it? Maybe Trillin had failed. Maybe she'd just given the old Endless a new trick.

Her fist clenched over the gesture for a fireball; her mind shaped it, the magic was ready to burn – but her other hand was still lit up.

And something in the translucent depths was *not the Endless.*

She didn't know how she knew. She didn't know if it was knowledge, or a twisted knot of hope and dread and heartbreak.

But if there was still something in there that was still her Trillin…

In the absence of any other sound, Trillin's voice twined up through her memories again.

Too reckless. You won't let anything stop you.

She never did. She rushed in. Headfirst. Fireball first. And it had always turned out fine. Nothing she couldn't blast or bluster or slice her way out of on the edge of a silver sword – hell. They'd escaped that world, but was there a part of it in her, still? The way Trillin thought there was a part of the Endless, somewhere in her ancestry?

She'd been thinking a lot about monsters recently. And not just the hot one who kept saving her life.

About witches, too. About magic. About being something that hid itself from its own world, in the bowels of a pocket dimension she had long ago stopped questioning. About being something that *needed* the world it hid itself from, as much as it feared it.

Did the world need them, too?

Or were they all just a fragment of something that wanted to consume everything it saw?

Trillin had made herself into something beautiful.

What had they made themselves into?

What did she want to be?

The answer was all around her.

She plunged her hands into the Endless, and it gave around her. Her right hand was still all lit up, and the light pulsed through the Endless's translucent flesh, red and pink and lavender-gold.

A tentacle wrapped around her wrist, and pulled her in.

Matter surrounded her, muscular and gelled, tendinous strands hauling her deeper. This was everything she'd risked, exploring the Endless in the first place, only this time she knew what it was that had captured her.

Trillin's voice echoed at the edge of her hearing. Wordless warnings, fond frustration. But *her.* A her that still existed separate from the whole.

For now.

The same way Sian still existed separate from everything around her. It wormed at her skin, trying to find a way in. One more bit of proof that whatever change Trillin had wrought on the Endless, what it was now wasn't solely *her.* Trillin had always been so careful of her edges. So polite about edging her way past Sian's.

She clenched a fist, ready to burn the way clear, but again, Trillin's words stopped her.

If this was the end of the world, maybe it could be the start of another one.

A better one. Less fucked up, maybe. Or if that was still too much to hope for…

Different.

She let her fingers open.

The Endless slipped in between every cell in her body.

It planted roots in her lungs. Felt its way to the cavity in her chest and built a nest there. And it still wasn't her. It wasn't either of them.

It was something new.

But here, lost in the midst of it, she could live by its rules. Briefly.

You're not what I'm looking for, she told it, opening her trachea to peel out the taproot. *And I'm not what you're looking for, either*, she added, scratching under her skin to dislodge experimental scales. *I'm here for…*

A woman who hadn't figured out how legs worked yet.

Who was delighted when she discovered a new type of joint to investigate.

Who was curious and tentative, joyous and bashful, straight-forward and strangely coy.

Who rebuilt herself every second of the day, and was always herself.

Whose thoughts bled into everything that was trying to make Sian a part of itself, and who was really bloody annoyed Sian had thrown herself in after her, when she *specifically said*, "*You weren't meant to come in here after me!*"

Sian laughed with relief. Everything that was Trillin pulled herself from the mass, shedding it like a diving bird sheds the ocean from its feathers.

And there was enough of the Endless left in Sian that she heard the echoes of Trillin's thoughts as she pulled herself together and apart.

Her fear. Her joy. Her *jealousy*, that the Endless she'd created would take the woman she loved like that, when she would *never*.

Trillin hauled herself into being and hauled Sian out with her, bursting out into open air that had never been so thin and light and sweet. A few stray tendrils tried to join them; she slapped them away.

"Stop that! Leave her alone." Trillin faced Sian, and whatever she'd taught the Endless about not devouring everything it was not, it was clear she'd learnt something from it in return.

Sian could see her, at last.

The monster she loved.

Glaring at her.

Filmy wings fluttered at Trillin's temples. "I said—"

"You did," Sian agreed.

"And you—"

"I listened to some of it." Sian kissed her. She was vaguely aware that she was breathing again, which was nice, and must mean that at some point she'd *stopped* breathing, which … anyway, she was breathing now. "Especially the important bit."

"The bit where you were meant to stay *outside* of it?"

"The bit about being kind to whatever came out when you didn't." She kissed her again, because, based on previous experience, they would shortly run out of opportunities for kissing. "Making sure you're the one who came out was the kindest thing I could do for the rest of it."

"You weren't meant to—"

"Follow you? I'll always follow you. And I'm not even going to pretend I'm sorry." She grinned. "Not sure slapping the new baby Endless fragments away from me counts as *kind*, though."

"You are not theirs," Trillin said, her eyes like distant galaxies and like home. "You're mine."

"Yes," Sian said. And, because it wasn't looking like Trillin would ever ask: "*Please.*"

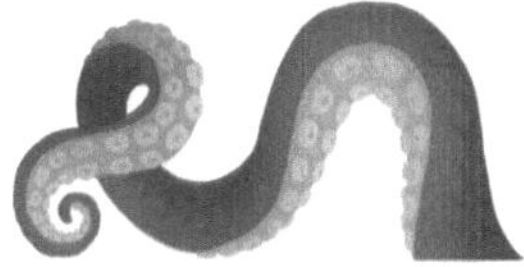

For one clutching heartbeat, they stood together beneath the broken stars, and then Trillin rushed in like the tide, filling the space she'd thrown the Endless out of, worry in every pulsing touch.

How long had it been, since she'd first imagined exploring the mysteries beneath Sian's flesh? The first time she'd seen her, vividly alive within the confines of her own body – a body that didn't confine her at all, but defined her. Joints and organs and blood, a deep forest of flesh, as strange to Trillin as Trillin's world and body must have been to Sian.

She pressed herself against Sian's skin, gentle and cutting as a thought. Sian hissed in a breath.

"Careful," Sian gasped, and Trillin stopped.

Laughter thrummed from Sian's body to hers; then a kiss, then more words. "I said *careful.* Not *stop.*"

She shivered with giddy delight.

"You want to make sure you got the rest of it out of me? Is that what this is?"

"And that," Trillin admitted, and this time, Sian's laughter was more of a cackle.

"All right, then."

She concentrated – beheld and held herself, everything she had made – and became something that could become something else.

Flesh like mist, form like shadow – she breathed herself into the pores of Sian's skin, the ducts and passageways, through blood and damp and heat. But kept herself *herself*, too, a body with arms that held Sian close as she explored her more intimately than any fragment of the Endless had ever explored any living piece of humanity.

The Endless devoured. It lunged, destroyed, made a husk and planted itself within, churning blood and moving limbs it did not understand. Trillin was a whisper in the breeze, a haunting, delicate and sure.

Sian breathed around her, ribs hitching, heart thudding – but not afraid.

There was so much of her. And each piece of her had been her for so long, bone and blood and organ, flesh and hair and her *mind*, the shimmer and sheen of wet hot electric impulse that held her soul in cupped and dancing hands.

Easier to destroy than to understand. Easier to devour and make her own, than risk destroying by accident, risk having all this wonder in her grasp and not being worthy of holding it.

Was that what the other Trillin had thought, when she tried to join with Sian, and lost herself to the thing Sian became?

Careful. She had to be careful. She knew too much of herself – too many of her selves – not to be wary of what she might become.

"What did you do in there?" Sian asked. It was strange, hearing Sian's words through her own senses and humming through Sian's own skull and flesh. And intriguing, too. There was so much more in her words from inside; a rustle of heat beneath the wondering.

"In *here*?" Trillin asked, within her.

Sian laughed. "In the Endless. After you went in, changed it, the fighting stopped. I could look at it again without being afraid or entranced. I could look at it without feeling – *anything*. It was like you made it you but *not* you, because if it was still you I would have felt something." There was something else beneath her words, now. Not heat, but dried and shrivelled from it.

Trillin cosied in closer. "I remembered for it. Everything it had forgotten."

"Everything we *theorised* it had forgotten. We didn't know for sure."

"But it worked. As soon as we – it – remembered what it had lost – it didn't need to devour you to rediscover it, again." Did Sian hear it, feel it, the mingled smugness and apology that twined around her words? "And it had already devoured so many humans, we – *it* only had to look closer into them to see what we'd been missing all along!"

Sian groaned, but it was laughter, as well, clenching at her ribs and huffing from her throat. And Trillin was in it all.

"And in me?" Sian asked. "Found anything astray?"

She hunted through Sian for anything that didn't belong, but it was all her. There was no worming fragment of the Endless hiding in her marrow. Whatever was left of the Endless in Sian's people was part of them now, not something separate to be pulled apart and away.

And nothing new, either. Nothing that remembered being Trillin and wanted *her* beloved – she had been careful, when she tore herself and Sian free, to take with her all *those* thoughts from the main bulk of the Endless, but if there were any hiding in Sian still…

She searched further. Dimly aware of Sian's fingers twitching, in the distance at the edges of her senses and Sian's body, she rearranged herself, rebuilt her senses to find not only Sian's body but her mind as well, and—

Found the Endless. Not a worm or a protein or a single atom, but a memory that showed her herself, a thousand times over, brutalising everything she touched.

She froze and Sian breathed around her.

"That's not the memory I was hoping you'd find," Sian said.

Trillin couldn't say anything.

After a moment, Sian added, "That wasn't you."

But it was.

"It wasn't," Sian repeated. "I'm not saying it might not have been, in other worlds."

Trillin had always been the horror. She'd seen it in countless eyes. But now, wrapped in a human's form – in *her* human's form – she felt it as never before. An encroaching gulf within her, hollowing her from the inside.

"I know." Sian's calm voice didn't help.

Trillin found enough of herself still outside Sian's body to speak. "Some of the other versions of me that you saw—"

"Weren't you."

"But they are almost me. They are *so close* to being me. Only a few days' difference, or a handful of decisions, or less—"

"None of them are as much you as you are." Breath hissed between Sian's teeth, into the narrowed confines of her too-tight chest. "We're both capable of things we don't want to be true. Whether that's the human or the Endless in us doesn't matter. Because they *don't have to be true.* Remember? We get to choose." She huffed a breath out through her nose. "If we didn't, we wouldn't have gotten into this mess. Or out of it. I chose you, and this is where we are now."

Sian licked her lips, and Trillin was in her tongue and teeth and throat. "You showed me how afraid you were, so you should know, there's one thing that was worrying me. About the hunger the Endless had for Earth. The hunger we had for it. What if when that went away, what I felt for you went away, too? What if I opened my eyes and it turned out the monster I wanted to fuck was inside me the whole time?"

Sian held her breath, poised on the edge of a precipice, and Trillin was there with her.

Too close to her heart to miss a single beat.

"You…" Everything Trillin was narrowed with suspicion. "You are *joking*? Now? You are telling jokes?"

"Can't it be true and a joke? We saved the world, Trillin. Out there. It's all saved. *Both* of them, yours and mine. We saved the worlds, we got the girl – what else is left except telling jokes about it?"

"You *got the girl*?" Trillin unwound and reformed herself mostly outside Sian again, who looked damp and slightly flushed.

"You, too." She gave a crooked, cocky grin. "Congrats. And it wasn't only a joke, by the way. Part of me was worried…"

She lifted a hand to Trillin, caressed her face, stared into her eyes with wonder and joy and relief.

Trillin held her hand there. "You were truly worried that what you feel for me isn't real?"

"I have a bad history with this sort of thing."

"And now you have a good future. And *the girl*. And…" Her hand came up, fingers gently caressing, touch following sight. She let Sian's gasp buoy her back into her own body, fully; then sank down again, found her way back into Sian, in a hundred delightful ways.

Sian's pupils expanded, and the change made the colour in her irises twitch the way humans' eyes never had before in this world, when faced with the Endless. Big and black and longing.

Trillin moved closer. "And I can think of better things to do after saving the world than *joke*."

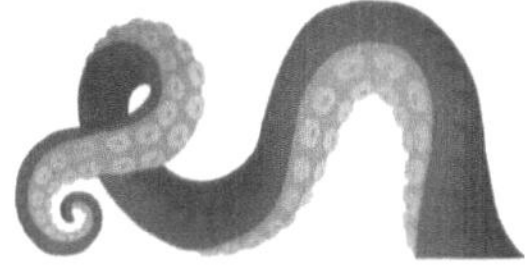

In a thousand realities, a thousand spiderwebbing choices led to something else.

Here, they led to this.

They'd saved the world. It took a while for that to sink in. They'd saved the world and, while the next few days and weeks involved a fair amount of discreet prodding so it stayed that way, for the most part it *kept itself* saved.

Even if what it was now was something nobody had expected or, really, knew what to do with.

The world Sian knew lurched anew, adjusting to the weight of the Endless sprawled through it, while the Endless adjusted to the strangeness of being somewhere instead of being everything. Part of it remained in its previous dimension, comforting itself with the familiar while other parts of it extended far into the strange and unyielding land.

Strange, except where it was familiar. Unyielding, except where it yielded. Most of the intrusion clustered around the coast, an echo of the volcanic eruption that had shaped the peninsula long before any human or other mind had been here to see it. Some ventured further. Some kept its changeability, while other tendrils hardened, slowed and became still in the way this world was – which was only really still to those too fast-moving to see the life in it.

Some sheared off and became things and people of their own, feeling strangely like this was not the first time they had done so.

Importantly, nobody had yet figured out that Sian was responsible for any of it.

And there was the other thing. The thing that meant Sian spent most of the next weeks at home, where for the first time her family saw her properly when they looked at her, and remembered what they'd seen when they looked away.

Whatever magic made the unmagical people of this world forget it existed the moment they stopped seeing it was gone. Like it had never been magically wiping people's minds in the first place.

Of course, that came with its own problems.

"Don't tell me this is *it*?" Flora was washing dishes, but less expensively than usual. When she dropped them, her magic looped down and grabbed them before they shattered on the floor. "Witches in the rest of the world thought you lot were weird enough before this, and now we've got an alien dimension literally taking root in our backyard and your lot's plan is, what? Bicker about it?"

"It's more like an old relative coming back from an overseas holiday that got out of hand. Thought you'd be more sympathetic. Anyway, what d'you mean, they all thought we were weird?"

Flora stared at her. "Would you believe there's a whole world out there that was *not* obsessed with building a creepy underground complex that allows them to study an eldritch dimension hell-bent on devouring all humanity?"

"What do they do all day, then? And, rude. That's our new neighbours you're talking about." Sian caught a mug as Flora flung it at her. "I'm more interested in how you ended up stuck with your ex as a—"

"I'm not answering questions about that," Flora said snippily.

"Meow!"

"And don't you start!"

Sian dug a little deeper. "Just think. If you'd waited a few more weeks, you wouldn't have needed to hijack Mal's magic in order to see what the coven was up to. If that's what you did."

"Ugh." Flora's expression darkened even further. "Don't remind me."

"Meow *meow*?"

"Sian?" Trillin called from the next room. "I am trying to bring the rest of the dishes, but the table keeps coming with me."

"Are you wrapped around it again?" Sian poked her head around the door. "You're wrapped around it again, love."

"Oh!"

"Need help getting untangled?"

"...Yes?"

Sian grinned as she abandoned the dishes. Trillin had grown more comfortable in her individuality since the Endless became part of the world. She was less wary of her edges. More liable to weave herself into the fabric of whatever piece of reality she found herself in proximity to, and more confident in her ability to unweave herself and *only* herself when she was done.

"You've got some of yourself in the monstera, too." Sian's Aunt Helen pointed with her phone, then gasped. "Monstera! Plants! Sian, there was something about plants. One Christmas, a few years ago?"

"I can't remember anything about trees at Christmas," Sian said as she knelt beside Trillin. Trillin gave her a bashful smile.

"You don't need to help untangle me," she said.

"It has its advantages." Sian grinned, teasing out tendrils from the wickerwork coffee table and re-tangling them around her own fingers.

Helen hummed. "That's right, you weren't here. Maybe Christine remembers. Oh, blast," she muttered as she tried to dip a gingernut biscuit into her tea and tap out a message on her phone at the same time, and dripped soggy crumbs onto the screen. "Could do with being able to grow a few extra fingers sometimes. You're lucky there, Trillin."

A half-dozen eyes snuck a half-dozen sly looks at Sian. "I am," she agreed.

Of everything that had happened, it was the reaction of her fellow humans, witch and not, that surprised Sian the most.

It was as though not only the world and all its magic, but all its people too, had jerked awake from a daydream and remembered with a sigh what they were. As though, all along, their reality should have encompassed the Endless and humanity both, and things finally felt … right.

Everyone was finally home.

"Meow!" The cat leapt onto the windowsill, its tail lashing.

"That's very helpful, Mal, but it would be more helpful if I could understand you." Helen clucked her tongue. "Wait – somewhere around here—" She balanced her tea, biscuit and phone in one hand, digging under the sofa with the other. "Here! Try these."

She threw a bag of Bananagrams at the cat, who stared at them in feline disgust. "Rrrrrrr."

"I can't hear you!" Flora carolled from the kitchen.

"What's that outside?" Helen stood up, peering out the window Mal was guarding. "Is there someone out there?"

Sian and Trillin exchanged a wary look.

The aftermath of the almost-end-of-the-world hadn't required a lot of tidying. But it had needed *some.*

"I'll go and have a look," Sian offered.

"Nonsense." Helen clacked her teacup down on the windowsill. "It's another little fragment, wandered in from that outcropping on the corner and now it can't figure out how to get back out the garden gate. They're always having trouble with doors and anything else with a hinge, poor things. I'll go and set it right."

"Are you sure?"

"Pff, Sian. It's not as though they're *dangerous.*"

She bustled out, already glowing with satisfaction that she was about to explore a part of this new world that none of her friends had yet managed, even if they did remember what had happened with the plants that Christmas.

Sian idled her way to the window anyway. Just to keep an eye on things.

"She's right, you know." Trillin followed her, tendrils still tangled in her fingers, a kite of contentment. "These new fragments aren't dangerous."

"We've got you to thank for that. And honestly? I'm surprised my lot haven't gone on the attack anyway." She frowned. "And not just my lot. The whole world suddenly remembered magic exists, and they don't freak out about it?"

"Your whole world remembers what magic is." Trillin leant against her, soft breath in her hair. "It remembers what *it* is. You feel it, too."

She did. "I'm hardly a good gauge for what's normal."

"Perhaps you are a better one than you think."

Outside, Helen approached the fragment, and led it gently by what might soon become an elbow back towards the gate. Inside, the cat picked up the Bananagrams bag and dragged it into the kitchen.

"I don't think anyone needs us in here," Sian suggested.

Trillin wisped closer to her. "I am not stuck to the table anymore."

"Want to get stuck to something else?"

Sian's rooms over the garage were just as she'd left them. Untidy, dusty and with holes eaten through the furniture from that first and only night she'd brought Trillin home before.

She couldn't even look at her, then. Now she couldn't do anything else. She was home, with the woman she loved. The monster who held her heart in her many-tendrilled hands.

They fell together at the top of the stairs, undid one another and discovered new ways to remake themselves the same way the world remade itself around them – slowly, joyfully, *home.*

Not a happy ever after, but happiness, ongoing. A world that had just rediscovered itself.

And she couldn't wait to discover it. Her and Trillin. Monsters, together.

AUTHOR'S NOTE

And there we have it: the final book in the Monster Girlfriend trilogy. Sian and Trillin's story is complete for now; frankly, I'm sure they're more than ready for a break. No more world-ending excitement, please. Let them catch their breath for a minute without the universe turning on its head. Again. Right before it drops a dragon on them.

When I first started writing what would become *How to Get a Girlfriend (When You're a Terrifying Monster)*, I had no idea I would end up writing three stories about this chaotic couple – or that their adventures would find so many readers. So thank you, all of you out there who've picked up these books and followed along with Sian and Trillin's love story and associated disasters. Special thanks also to my fmaily, for your unwavering support; and my writing friends, particularly AJ and Mel, for bearing up beneath the constant onslaught of my uncertainties and grumblings. Don't worry. There's more where that came from.

Word-of-mouth is the best support an indie author can receive. If you enjoyed *How to Get the Girl (And Not Destroy the World)*, I would love if you left a review letting other readers know what to liked about it.

Want to hear when I have a new book coming out? You can sign up to my newsletter at www.mariecardno.com.

Until next time,

Marie

ALSO BY MARIE CARDNO

The Monster Girlfriend Trilogy

How to Get a Girlfriend (When You're a Terrifying Monster)

How to Get a Date with the Evil Queen

How to Get the Girl (And Not Destroy the World)

www.ingramcontent.com/pod-product-compliance
Lightning Source LLC
Chambersburg PA
CBHW030146010826
48973CB00002B/745

* 9 7 8 1 9 9 1 1 9 6 8 5 9 *